MY DAD

CHAPTER 1

Arjun came to his mother's room early in the morning. It must be around 7 O' clock when light from the sun reached to the room through the casement. Arjun's mother remained lying motionless on the bed and he stood in awe, that why she didn't rise early this day as it was she who rouses him from sleep every day. His mother Kaveri, used to rise early in the morning and wake her husband and her only son and she gave them something to drink; but today, her husband rose earlier than her and went into the bathroom.

Arjun approached his mother.

"Mother...mother," he called her.

He had misgivings as to why his mother didn't rise early in the morning and he fretted something as headache or something like that must have happened to her as normally, she rises like this some days, when she is affected with some ailments such as fever, cough, etc. Arjun wanted to know whether she has got any disease as Kaveri was lying facing downwards and so, her face was not to be seen.

"Mother...mother," Arjun called her once again, this time a bit louder. There was no response.

"Mum, wake up," he said again when at the same time, his father came out of the bathroom, which was attached to that bedroom, where the couples slept. Arjun turned to his father on seeing him partially.

"Didn't your mother rise yet? Arjun's father, Ashok Kumar asked him on catching sight of both of them.

"No dad. I called her. I think she is ill."

Ashok Kumar closed in on his wife.

"Kaveri...Kaveri," he tried to awaken her. He called her several times, but, there was no any response. Both the father and the son made her shudder, holding her and called her loudly. Ashok Kumar turned her slowly as facing upwards; they were stunned, seeing her face. It seemed as if she is dead. Both father and son looked at each other in great anguish when Arjun was about to bawl.

"What happened to her, father? What happened to her?"

He was as if he couldn't believe himself and he was petrified. Ashok Kumar too was not of a different condition that tears rolled from his eyes. He checked whether she could breathe and found that she had stopped respiring. He closed her eyes, which were open, patting on them when Arjun burst into tears and was paralysed altogether and was trying to hold his dead mother tightly by his arms. Ashok Kumar too was weeping and he too felt as if immobilized. Both of them cuddled Kaveri and cried for long, being not able to accredit that she is ceased to be alive and that they cannot see her any more.

"What is the cause of her death, father?" after a while Arjun asked his father.

"I don't know my boy. She had slept yesterday night just as every other night. She had no any mess whatsoever or, at least, she had not intimated me about anything special," Ashok Kumar said, looking at Arjun's filled eyes.

Ashok Kumar and Arjun knew that she had had cardiac arrest two times before and they thought that it would be the reason for her death that it must have occurred to her the last night.

"Must be, she had a heart disease last night," Ashok Kumar added after a small pause.

Arjun said nothing, but hugged his father, being not able to stand the grief.

"Arjun, now we have to inform everybody and perform her last rites," Ashok Kumar said long after remaining in that position, clasping his son.

They were sitting in the bed, embracing each other after piping their eyes for a long time and they stood up later, still looking at the motionless body of Kaveri.

" Let me apprise our relatives and neighbours, giving them a bell. You stay here," Ashok Kumar moved to another room saying thus.

Arjun embraced his mother after his father left and he sobbed loudly with a heavy heart that he had loved his mother so much.

"Arjun, neighbours are coming. I am going to the front," Ashok Kumar came to Arjun and put into words after he talked by telephone.

"Okay dad."

Arjun got to his feet slowly, leaving his mother and he tried to show some maturity, which is not to be found much in a boy of his age. Arjun came to the forepart of the domicile after a while and he saw a neighbour talking to his father. When they looked at him, they felt commiseration for the boy.

"Arjun," Alok, who was their nearest neighbour called Arjun.

He was of Ashok Kumar's age and one of his best friends. Arjun tried to simper to him but did not speak anything. Alok came to him and consoled him, putting his left arm on his right shoulder. In the meanwhile, more persons living next doors came to the dwelling and now there are twelve persons besides Alok, gathered there coming from the four houses located nearby. Other houses were far-flung from their house. All of them came inside the house to see the dead body and they comforted Arjun and his father. Ashok Kumar and Arjun did not show much sorrow outwardly, but tried to be friendly outward.

Ashok Kumar's kinsmen and kinswomen came as time passed, thus, the house and its surroundings are filled with visitors now and those who came, saw the cadaver. They felt sympathy for Ashok Kumar and Arjun and felt sad to lose Kaveri. They knew that Kaveri wasn't of old age that she was only thirty eight years old and they thought, how unlucky the father and son are to lose their beloved so early in life.

Arjun's eyes were all wet of tears; he tried to be away from others. He sat in his bed in his room and mourned and those who gathered there intentionally left him alone as they thought it might be appropriate for the occasion. Ashok Kumar mingled with the people, crying inside his mind.

Time passed and the body was to be taken to the funeral. Some of the neighbours and relatives came forward to take the body to burn as it was their custom to do so and the corpse was taken outside the house and the people converged there followed it to a ground, which was nearby. Arjun and Ashok Kumar too were among the crowd.

The horde reached the terrain and after sometime, the body was placed over a pyre. Arjun ignited Kaveri's body as people looked to. The flames soared high in the air. Arjun saw his mother's body being taken by the blaze through his wet eyes and he became weary. The recognition that he has to live the rest of his life without his mother was unbearable to him. Ashok Kumar had loved his wife than anything else that he too felt it tiresome to live without her.

After the last rites, many of the multitude dispersed, who were mainly the natives who had come in large numbers and many of the relatives and neighbours returned to Ashok Kumar's house along with him and Arjun. Arjun's schoolmates and Ashok Kumar's colleagues had come to the funeral, they too returned to the house. Arjun locked his room from inside and reclined on the bed as soon as they got as far as the abode. He then, lay facing downwards pressing his head on the bolster and he shed tears for long, remaining in that state while Ashok Kumar carried on with those, present there.

Time still elapsed and almost everyone broke up as the dusk came and darkness was going to devour that part of the earth when Arjun seemed to be relieved after crying for a long time and he came out of the room to his father and when he saw him, he was talking to his brother. All the three brothers and one sister of Ashok Kumar had come; their families and brothers and sisters of Kaveri with their families had also come. The relatives of the parents of Ashok Kumar and Kaveri had come too, but not their parents themselves, as they were not in this world. When Ashok Kumar's brothers, sisters and others saw Arjun, they directed their eyes at him and smiled and Arjun also simpered to them back as he had hearty attachment with all of his relatives.

"Arjun, come and have something. Aren't you hungry?" The wife of Ashok Kumar's eldest brother asked him, smiling to him.

"I don't want anything now. I shall have it afterwards," Arjun said.

He had not eaten anything much from the morning that he hadn't ravenousness. He is not interested now in anything, rather, he is preoccupied with the thoughts of his mother. He spent almost an hour with others. They were like any other relatives who loved every other and frequently visited everyone. Later, all of them dispersed, some going to their residences and some staying there itself and Arjun and Ashok Kumar hit the sack.

It had become 7 o' clock in the morning when Ashok Kumar got up. He had slept with Arjun last night in his room, where he slept with his wife earlier. When he looked at Arjun, he was   slumbering; he looked the adolescent at his face.

"Poor boy, how unlucky it is to lose one's mother in this age," Ashok Kumar said to himself.

Ashok Kumar rose from the bed, stood up and he looked at Arjun affectionately. He never liked his son to be woebegone, that he used to fulfil any of his wishes and he had loved his son so much that he could not bear seeing this condition of him. The marks of tears which flowed through his cheeks were still there on his visage. The beams of the sun had entered the room in which they slept last night. Ashok Kumar did not try to wake Arjun. He thought of waking him after some time so that he can be free from the pangs of bereavement of his mother at least for that time and he touched Arjun with his lips on the forehead. He went to the bathroom later.

Time elapsed. The rest of the kinsfolk who slept in that house went to their houses after having breakfast. Arjun, after eating bread, butter and jam with his father, went to his father's room after his relatives departed when after sometime Ashok Kumar came to him to that room and sat on the bed beside Arjun. Arjun had become recumbent on the bed and Ashok Kumar patted on his back as he was lying facing downwards as he knew how much his son is suffering.

Now that, Ashok Kumar and Arjun are alone in that house, they spent time not expressing anything in spoken words to each other. Ashok Kumar had doted on his only son to a great extent that he had got him after years' waiting that Arjun was born after five years from the day of his marriage with Kaveri. For that very reason, he loved his son more than any other parent, loved his child. Ashok Kumar and his wife had seen Arjun as a precious jewel and it was such that they brought him up and they tried to fulfil all of his ambitions. In fact, the couples had loved their son more than they loved each other and Arjun too loved them back with the same intensity. He held his parents dear above anything else that he was not able to part them for even a day.

Now, both of them loved each other than earlier. It was such that they felt the love they had for Kaveri also to one another. Arjun felt for his father more love than the love he had towards him before the demise of his mother.

Arjun looked at his father, raising his head from that position of lying facing downwards and Ashok Kumar saw Arjun looking at him.

"Arjun, stand up and sit here beside me," Ashok Kumar said to Arjun, looking compassionately at his downcast face.

Arjun stood up unhurriedly and sat beside Ashok Kumar.

"How do you feel now?" Ashok Kumar inquired after him, putting his right arm on his left shoulder.

"Feeling better," Arjun responded.

Thenceforth, they did not speak much. Arjun embraced his father and they continued in that position for long.

"Dad, I am going to bathe," saying thus Arjun stood up after a while.

"Okay, go and bathe," Ashok Kumar enunciated freeing him.

Ashok Kumar and Arjun stood up simultaneously; Arjun went to bathe and Ashok Kumar went to the portico. They have begun to live as before after the death of Kaveri, but still, the minds of them were at all times occupied with the thoughts of their beloved.

CHAPTER 2

Two weeks passed by. Till now, Arjun and Ashok Kumar had not gone outside the house much after the demise of Kaveri but stayed indoors most of the times and it has become two weeks after they last went to school as the father and the son went to the same academy as one was a teacher there and the other a student. By now, their grief of losing their beloved has decreased to an extent and they have made up their minds to go to school this day after two weeks' leave. It is a Wednesday today. Arjun had got bathing done and had had his breakfast as Ashok Kumar too had become prepared to go to school.

"Shall we go, Arjun?" Hearing Ashok Kumar's words, Arjun came to his room carrying his schoolbag.

"Yes dad, we shall go," Arjun said.

The time was nine fifteen and the school started at ten. Ashok Kumar and Arjun came out of their house and Ashok Kumar locked the door. He too had a bag with him. After locking the door, Ashok Kumar came near to his car, where Arjun had reached as early as this. The car had been parked in front of the house on the left side in a shed. It was a car of about five lakh rupees, blue in colour, Swift of Maruti Suzuki company, to be precise. Father and son got into the car without delay after Ashok Kumar unlocked and opened its door and both of them seated themselves in the front seats. They did not speak a thing. After a while, the car got started and moved forward as it was already kept in a direction so as to take it forward without taking reverse. Arjun had opened the gate already. Ashok kumar took the car in the direction he faced, to the main road, passing their compound, as their house was located near the main road that stretched in front of their house.

The car darted through the road to their school, which was not very distant from their house. They could reach the school by a running of fifteen minutes. People looked at Arjun and Ashok Kumar as both of them were strikingly handsome and there were many of them who knew them personally and they smiled to them. Arjun was beholding the sights; he kept mum throughout the journey. Neither Ashok Kumar did speak a word. Arjun was pondering how happy he was when he went to school earlier like this, when his mother was alive. She used to do everything for him to prepare him to go to school that she would garb him in his uniform, put the tiffin box in his bag and put the appropriate books in his bag as per the time table every day before he went to school. Her remembrances brought tears into his eyes.

It had become nine forty when they reached the school. They descended from the car after parking it where teachers   temporarily left their vehicles and walked to the school building.

"Arjun, you first see your class teacher and then go to your class room," Ashok Kumar turned to Arjun and said to him somberly.

"Yes, dad" Arjun said, shaking his head vertically.

"Then, see you in the evening," Ashok Kumar said to Arjun thus, because there was no much chance of them meeting each other before evening.

This day, Ashok Kumar did not have to take class to Arjun as he had all other days to take classes to him. Ashok Kumar took classes in English for Arjun and on Wednesdays, it was another instructor, who took classes to him.

"See you dad," Arjun moved away from Ashok Kumar as Ashok Kumar stopped there to talk to one of his colleagues.

"See you too," he said.

Arjun saw his class teacher and talked to him. He had been informed before itself about the death of his student's mother.

Arjun set foot in his class room. All his classmates looked at him sympathetically when they saw him and he smiled to them and they smiled to him back. Arjun went to his seat and sat there when everybody watched him. Many of the students went to him in a consoling manner; they talked to him. His close friends with whom he spent time normally came to him from outside as they had gone to see their another companion. They talked to him pacifying words. Many of Arjun's classmates had come to his house to attend the funeral.

After some time, the class teacher came to the classroom and he said good morning to the students and they to him back, then, all of them stood respecting him. The teacher asked them to sit down and they obeyed him. The teacher whose name was George asked Arjun something about him concerning his mother's death and Arjun spoke to him as other students gazed at him. Then, he began to take class. His subject was maths. He asked some students, questions from what he taught them the previous day and the students answered them correctly. Then, he taught the students, the day's lessons.

When interlude came after two hours Arjun went out of the classroom with his close friends. He had several acquaintances in the school other than those in his classroom. Arjun was the top mark scorer in the examinations in the whole school and thus teachers loved him much because of this and because his father being their colleague. Everybody looked at Arjun pathetically as he passed by them through the corridor as everybody in that school knew about Arjun's mother's death and some of them talked to him when he came at hand to them.

Arjun and his confidants came out of the school building; they went to a cool bar where there were other students. They sat inside the cool bar. As it was Wednesday, students had not worn their uniform as on Wednesdays they hadn't to wear uniform and it is a delight to watch them wearing their Sunday best. Boys wore shirts and pants of different colours and designs whereas girls wore mainly salwar kameezes, pants and shirts and all of them tried to impress others, especially the opposite sex. Boys and girls flirted as many of the students were lovers and they found it very interesting to seek love from the opposite sex. The students were very jolly the other days when they were not aware of the plight of Arjun. Arjun too was a playful teenager earlier. He too had a lover, Pooja. That was her name. Arjun's friends knew their relationship and they would call him in jest, her name. She was very beautiful and matching to Arjun.

Now, nobody spoke much, contrary to the former atmosphere out there as earlier, the school compounds used to be filled with the shouting and guffaw of the students, especially the boys. They talked about everything. They were fans of film stars and sports stars and they argued for particular celebrities of whom they were fans, while Arjun too stood by his idols and talked on behalf of them. He was a fan of Shah Rookh Khan and Rahul Dravid.

Many of them did not play cricket or football in these short intervals as they got little time to play, but they played them during the noon after lunch or in the evening. As it was a high school, many of the students were of Arjun's age. Arjun studied in the eighth standard. He was a terrific fast bowler and an ordinary batsman and other students feared his pace when he bowled to them. Some days, Arjun did not return to his house in the evening with his father in the car, but played cricket with his friends and went home later.

Pooja was talking to Arjun when they were to return to the classroom after the interval that she felt very sorry for Arjun that he has been taken away his mother from him forever and Arjun's close friends were with him then. Pooja was their classmate. They moved to their classroom, conversing to each other when all the boys and girls returned to their classrooms when the bell rang for the next hour as it was a good sight to see them moving to the classrooms as a procession.

Time elapsed. The day's classes are over and Arjun had not seen his father until they met each other in the evening though in the midday, Ashok Kumar had seen Arjun from far when he came to the canteen for the lunch, but, Arjun did not perceive his father with the eyes and Ashok Kumar waited for Arjun near the car in the evening to go home where Arjun came to, without delay.

"Shall we go, Arjun?" Ashok Kumar asked Arjuin smilingly.

"Yes dad," saying thus Arjun opened the car's door and got in.

Ashok Kumar started the car and it moved forward after it had been taken reverse.

"How were today's classes?" Ashok Kumar asked Arjun as he steered the car.

"It was nice," said Arjun.

Thenceforth, they didn't speak much as the car ran through the highway in Worli, Mumbai as it was their place and the city was crowded with people, foreign and native.

"Arjun, do you want to go home or somewhere else?" Ashok Kumar asked Arjun after a while.

"Where?"

"Anywhere, you wish."

"Let us go to the beach then," Arjun looked at his father and said.

"Okay then," Ashok Kumar adhered Arjun.

Ashok Kumar moved the car after sometime so as to go to the left, where there was a road to the beach as both of them had a desire to be relieved from the agony due to the death of their beloved. Arjun, Ashok Kumar and Kaveri used to go to the beach occasionally, earlier. Arjun and Ashok

Kumar thought retrospectively about Kaveri as the car moved forward that she was a very loving   person that she loved her husband and son immensely. They used to go together to various places but the beach was where they visited frequently. Arjun felt as if his mother sitting in the back seat and he felt as if the motherly love pervaded all over there.

They arrived at the beach by 5 o'clock as they had set out   from the school when it was four fifteen and Arjun and Ashok Kumar descended from the car after parking it on the roadside. Ashok Kumar locked the car and he walked to the beach along with Arjun, where it was thronged with people and there were adults and children from various parts of India and abroad gathered there. The climate was good as there was no much heat or much coldness when both Ashok Kumar and Arjun walked through the sands on the beach and there was breeze over there in that evening. The horizon turned to red colour after some time and the sun had begun to set when Arjun looked at the sky and Ashok Kumar was looking at the vast sea at the same time. They, as others, thought that the almighty god would be somewhere there in the sky.

They bought a cup of coffee each with pizza from a nearby shop and they watched the people from that shop as they sat there. People were of different nationalities and there were many good looking men and women among them and many of them sat on the sands and others just strolled over it while Ashok Kumar and Arjun spent a lot of time in that pizza emporium after when they met some of their acquaintances in that shop and they talked to them for some time.

"Arjun, we can go home after having supper," Ashok Kumar said to Arjun when they came out of the shop.

"Okay dad," Arjun said as he knew that they would have to cook themselves the food, if they went home without dining.

They met one of Ashok Kumar's friends when they went further and Ashok Kumar spent time, talking to him. The friend, Dev asked something to Arjun and Arjun replied to him when many of the people looked at them as they stood near the sea. Arjun looked around to see the sights and he saw children mingling with their parents, and later, he saw one boy sitting on the lap of his mother and the mother touching him gently with the flat of her hand on his head. They were much near to Arjun and he looked at them for long with tears in his eyes.

By and by when it was 7 O'clock, they entered a delicatessen and ate supper, then, they returned to their house when it turned to be seven thirty when the sky turned to be dark as the sun had set already. Many of the people had begun to disperse as the car moved along with Ashok Kumar and Arjun to their house and both of them did not talk much to each other.

CHAPTER 3

This morning, Arjun woke earlier than his father and he got up from the bed and went to the bathroom after looking outside through the window, which was open the whole night and he did not wake his father that he thought that let him sleep till he comes from the bathroom. Ashok Kumar woke after some time just when Arjun came out of the bathroom.

"Dad, are you awake?" Arjun asked, seeing Ashok Kumar sitting on the bed.

"Yes dear," Ashok Kumar said, smiling.

"I will bring you tea by the time you come, brushing your teeth," Arjun said to Ashok Kumar in a loving manner.

Arjun did for his father such things regarding them as his duty in the absence of his mother. When Ashok Kumar came out of the bathroom, he saw his cup of tea on the teapoy, which was placed near the bed and Arjun came to him as he sipped the tea.

"Dad, aren't we going to the school, today?" Arjun asked his father, sitting in the bed near him.

"Yes, we have to," was Ashok Kumar's answer.

Later, they went to school. Like the last day, they parked the car in the fenced-in enclosure of the school and walked to the school building after they reached the school as Arjun went to his classroom and Ashok Kumar to the teacher's room.

Everything was like as yesterday. Unlike as yesterday, they returned home after the classes in the evening without going anywhere. One more day they went to the school. The grief still persisted in the minds of the father and the son as Ashok Kumar thought of going somewhere. His eldest brother worked in Qatar and he was there in Mumbai when Kaveri died and had come to her funeral and Ashok Kumar wished to visit him as by that he and Arjun may be able to forget the sorrow to some extent.

"Arjun, are you interested in going somewhere?" Ashok Kumar asked Arjun, when they were having their lunch, the next day.

It was Sunday and they had not gone to school. They had made the lunch themselves.

"Where to?" Arjun asked his father enthusiastically.

"To Qatar, where your uncle is," Ashok Kumar said, looking at Arjun in a mien denoting whether he liked his suggestion or not.

"Definitely dad, I was thinking this to tell you," Arjun spoke with expanded eyes as he too had thought of it.

"Then, we can take leave for one week from the school   after we got visa. You would get solace from your sorrow if you travel."

"Yeah."

Ashok Kumar finished eating and got up, then, he washed his hands and went to the portico. He took a magazine that was lying   on the teapoy. Arjun finished his eating and came to his father and he looked around while his father read the periodical, being seated on a chair. In front of their house, there was a ravishing garden of which the plants were planted by Arjun and his parents and there were beautiful flowers over the plants, of yellow, rose and red colours. Arjun looked at the garden, standing near his father. There were different kinds of plants in the cultivated ground, most of which were brought from distant places.

"Arjun, isn't there cricket live today?" Ashok Kumar asked Arjun after a while as though he suddenly thought about it.

"Yes dad, it will start at 2 o'clock," Arjun replied as it seemed he too was thinking about it.

"What is the time now?"

"It is one forty five now," Arjun looked at his watch and said.

Ashok Kumar got up from his seat and went to the guest room with Arjun, where television had been placed and Arjun switched on the TV and sat in front of it with his father as a match was to be held between India and Australia that day. After some time, the match   got commenced when it turned 2 o'clock before which there was a conversation between three old players who were the former Indian players, Sunil Gavaskar, Sanjay Manjarekar and Navajyoth Singh Siddu who had mentioned that the wicket is a batting track and the spectators are eager to watch as Saurav Ganguly and Sachin Tendulkar were going to open the innings for India.

Both Ashok Kumar and Arjun liked Saurav and Sachin. They cheered as Saurav took stance after taking guard, and later Australian opening bowler Glen Mc Grath came running to the bowling crease and delivered a fast ball after jumping slightly to take his bowling action and Saurav

Ganguly defended the good length ball with excellent timing. Captain Ricky Ponting had set the field very tight. The crowd of fifty thousand people at the Chepauk stadium at Chennai roared as Mc Grath came running for his second ball as for his first ball. Saurav defended that ball too. It was in the fifth ball of the over that Ganguly opened his account, it being a magnificent boundary on the off side from the bat of a batsman who owned a lazy elegant batting style as the fielders ran after the ball in vain.

The match progressed as Ashok Kumar and Arjun saw it eagerly opining about the happenings. Now, first ten overs are over when the scoreboard showed 65 for no loss. Sachin is on 25 and saurav on 34; Extras 6. India is in a strong position, having a head start, though as captain Ricky Ponting used all of his arrows in his quiver Sachin and Saurav was not to be tamed.

Spinners came and medium pacers came, but no wicket fell till the twentieth over and when Sachin fell on 56, India had attained a total of 139 on the scoreboard. Sachin became out in Shane Warne's ball as it hit the middle stump. It was a good total that the Indian batsmen would be hazardous in the coming overs as they had nine wickets left, but, the spectators were dejected when Sachin became out. Sachin walked to the pavilion acknowledging the cheers of the people for his half century. Then came Rahul Dravid and he along with Saurav Ganguly led India forward as they could keep the run rate at six runs per over and wicket did not fall until the fortieth over. Saurav Ganguly became out in Mc Grath's ball which was a short pitched one off which Saurav, a good timer of the ball as he is, tried to hit a six above mid wicket and it was Damien Fleming who took the catch. The score was 248 then and Saurav had scored a century, 113 runs. His fans greeted him with much warmth and thenceforth, Dravid and the new batsman, Mohammed Azharudheen tried to score runs prolifically as the crowd was all spurring the batsmen throughout the match. They were rapturous to see their idols in front of their eyes. When the Indian batting was over, one could read the scoreboard, the Indian total as 350 for 2. Azhar remained not out on 60 and Rahul not out on 101 and that was suffice for the Indian fans that their heroes have scored two centuries and two half centuries.

"Dad, it's five thirty now; I will bring you coffee," saying thus after some time, Arjun rose from his chair and stood before his father.

They had made their comments about the match when it was going on as Arjun and Ashok Kumar felt merry to see the Indian batsman scoring highly. Arjun opined that Australia was not going to win the match and Ashok Kumar backed his son.

"Yes dear," Ashok Kumar responded.

Arjun went to the kitchen as he had been accustomed to   cooking after his mother's death and his father helped him in his cooking. He made a delectable coffee adding Nescafe coffee powder, sugar and milk powder to the boiled water. He liked to make food and drinks for his father. Arjun came back to the room and placed the cup of coffee and a saucer containing some biscuits on the table and he went back to bring his coffee and then, the father and son imbibed the coffee and ate the biscuits together.

Time passed. Australian opening batsmen Mark Waugh and Adam Gilchrist walked to the batting crease as Ashok Kumar and Arjun along with the people from all over the world watched them   avidly on the television. Everybody anticipated the victory of the Indians as they thought, Australia would have to sweat to surmount   the huge total of India. Mark Waugh took guard and became ready to face Venketesh Prasad. Venketesh Prasad came running to him and delivered a good length ball and Mark Waugh defended the ball very well. He could score his first run in the fourth ball. Debashish Mohanty came after Prasad and both of them bowled very tightly that the Australian batsmen could not score much and after the first ten overs were over, Australia are 40 for none.

After the first ten overs, the Australian batsmen tried to score by leaps and bounds that the run rate rose to 5.3 when the first twenty overs were bowled. In the meanwhile, they lost two wickets of Mark Waugh and Ricky Ponting as Mark Waugh fell on 35 and Ricky Ponting on 24. Gilchrist took 37 runs. He is batting with Steve Waugh, who is on 4. There were a number of Australian fans in the stadium who were hopeful seeing the run rate rising whereas the Indian fans were apprehensive in the rising run rate as they feared that the Australians may slog in the coming overs, they having eight wickets in hand.

The Australians tried their level best to counterattack the Indians, but they fell through in it, reaching only to 320. They lost all the wickets in the attempt. The members of the victorious Indian team celebrated their triumph on the field by embracing each other when the crowd also enjoyed themselves, the success, making noise and waving their hands. The Australian tail enders walked to the pavilion amidst the Indian players.

Ashok kumar and Arjun saw the match till the end and it has become ten in the night when the day-night match was over and the presentation ceremony occurred later. Ashok Kumar and Arjun saw the whole nine yards till the end. Saurav Ganguly was adjudged as the man of the match and he spoke at the presentation area. Captain, Mohammed Azharudheen also spoke, realising his responsibility as his counterpart Ricky Ponting also said some words.

Arjun turned off the TV as everything was over. Now, they want something to eat; Arjun brought some chappathis and vegetable curry to the dining table. It was made by him, the previous day as they sometimes made the food in the house and sometimes bought from outside. Ashok Kumar and Arjun dined together and it had become eleven thirty when they went to bed and when they lay together, there was the bellowing of the crowd in their minds as they were in high spirits that India won the match.

Days passed. Ashok Kumar and Arjun went to school daily. They were still sad to lose their mother that Arjun thought about Kaveri always and the fact that he cannot see her anymore made him weary. They occasionally went to places like beach, cinema theatre, etc and most of the times, they ate food from outside and they visited their friends and relatives as they visited them before Kaveri's death.

Ashok Kumar's and Arjun's visa came later as they had applied for it earlier and Ashok Kumar decided to take leave from the school for one week. He told Arjun about that and the next day they went to school with that intention. They attended the classes in the forenoon and went back to their abode after taking leave before which Ashok Kumar had met the headmaster for taking the leave and had informed other teachers and many of his students about his leave.

They reached home. It was a lovely house with only one storey and the colour of the house was light brown and it was somewhat big with three bedrooms. Ashok

Kumar's car moved through the path in between the garden on both sides of the yard to the car shed, located on the left side of the house and Ashok Kumar turned the car in the direction of the car shed and took the car to the shed and parked it there. Father and son descended from the car and they moved to the house after Ashok Kumar locked the car.

They took tickets to Qatar to fly by Gulf air. The flight is on 6 o' clock in the dusk, the next Tuesday. Arjun and Ashok Kumar crammed their bags with their things on Tuesday, after the breakfast. They had to check in at the airport at 3 O' clock. They had bought two new holdalls earlier and they filled in them, their three dresses out of their four apparels. They had a hand bag too. They hadn't much other items to take to Qatar though they had bought food items that are not available at Qatar to give to Ashok Kumar's eldest brother, Vishal and his family.

Ashok Kumar and Arjun finished packing and they came out of the house at one thirty. Many of the neighbours, relatives and their acquaintances who had known earlier about Ashok Kumar's and Arjun's departure had come to say farewell to them. All of them had had their lunch earlier, including Arjun and Ashok Kumar. Ashok Kumar locked the door of the house and walked to the car with Arjun, they taking leave of everybody. They placed the luggage in the dickey of the car and ascended it with three of their relatives who accompanied them to the airport. Ashok Kumar steered the car as those who gathered there waved their hands to them smilingly and they, back. The car entered the main road after sometime as the gate had been opened earlier and it ran to the right, where the aerodrome was.

CHAPTER 4

It is Sahar International Airport, Mumbai. There are so many people congregated in the airport terminal while many of them are passengers and there are people who are not travellers among them who have come to send off and receive the passengers. It had become two forty when Ashok Kumar and Arjun reached the airport. They came near to the terminal and afterwards, parked the car in the parking area. One of the three relatives came with them was Ashok Kumar's nephew and other two were Arjun's cousins. All of them entered the airport terminal, and later, Ashok Kumar and Arjun checked in without delay.

They had to stay inside the airport for about three hours before ascending the plane. The employees inside the airport checked their luggage and they weighed it to know whether it exceeded the allowed weight limit. Ashok Kumar's and Arjun's relatives said them goodbye and remained outside until they ascended the plane. They bought cool drinks and potato chips. Later, after Ashok Kumar and Arjun boarded the plane, they returned.

Ashok Kumar's and Arjun's relatives went back in Ashok Kumar's car, which his nephew would keep with him till Ashok Kumar and Arjun come back to India as Ashok Kumar had asked him to do so. Arjun and Ashok Kumar boarded the aeroplane after some time. They are for the first time inside a plane that they had not travelled   by a plane hitherto. They had only travelled by car, train and bus inside India, being never travelled to a foreign country.

Arjun sat on a window seat in the right side of the plane and Ashok Kumar sat beside him. Almost all of the seats were occupied. There sat a young Punjabi man in the seat near to them seeming to be of about thirty years of age. He beamed to Ashok Kumar and Arjun and they smiled to him back. He seemed to be a talkative man. All the other passengers have seated themselves now that it seemed there is no one to come next. Arjun was looking outside through the porthole and he saw a part of the runway. He looked at the other passengers too when Ashok Kumar talked to the Punjabi man in English. He told Ashok Kumar that he is working at Qatar and he is going there as his leave of two months have expired. He is a construction engineer there working for a construction company in Doha. He introduced himself as Harbajan Singh from Patiala, Punjab and he asked the whereabouts of Ashok Kumar. Ashok Kumar introduced himself and Arjun to him, telling him their names and that they are from Mumbai and why they travelled to Qatar as he told him other things about them. Ashok Kumar saw the amiable man to be very pleasing and he thought that he has got a good company during the journey.

The plane is now going to take off before which the airhostesses had asked the passengers to tie their seatbelts. As travelling for the first time in an aeroplane, take off was a new experience to Ashok Kumar and Arjun though they had heard about it before. They fastened their seatbelts. After running very fast, the plane soared to the sky. Arjun and Ashok Kumar along with other passengers experienced a difficulty when the plane rose to height. They had heard about it beforehand from their acquaintances, who   had travelled by plane. Ashok Kumar and Arjun had seen the inside   of planes and airbases on YouTube and had known several things about them. They felt fear when the plane rose. The Sikh man, who knew that they are flying for the first time, looked at them to know how they experienced this. Ashok Kumar and Arjun showed him that they felt fear slightly.

"Don't worry. It will not last long," Harbajan Singh said.

Ashok Kumar and Arjun just smiled.

"When the plane reaches the heights, it would be alright. Then you can enjoy the journey in a plane," The Sikh man continued.

Ashok Kumar and Arjun smiled, but said nothing.

The plane reached the sky and the fearfulness is gone in the passengers. Arjun could see Mumbai city through the porthole, fading from him as the plane flew aloft. Now, he can see only clouds through the porthole though it was not visible clearly as darkness had pervaded outside the plane slightly. He showed his father, the sights outside the plane as it was a fabulous sight to see clouds from near which they had only seen from very low. The Sikh man too was watching the overcast from his seat.

After sometime, an airhostess came to them with sweets and she gave them to all passengers, for them to take from a tray. Arjun, Ashok Kumar and Harbajan Singh took a few of the chocolates. Eating the chocolates, Arjun took a magazine which he saw in front of him, kept in a pocket at the back of the front seat and he turned its pages. The magazine was exclusively for the passengers of Gulf Air, containing articles about special people and places amid a lot of advertisements. There were ads of apparels, cars, etc. Ashok Kumar and Harbajan Singh too took the in-flight magazines.

Later, when it was seven thirty, the airhostess fetched meals for them which were chicken biriyanies, dry fruits placed over them. Ashok Kumar and Arjun felt that it was different from the biriyani, they got outside after tasting which they ensured what they thought was right that it was different in appearance as well as in taste. They had seen different kinds of such food, available in planes, on YouTube. The three of them ate the food which was mouth watering and which had something special about it, different from the ordinary food, one could get outside the plane. There were three or four items of food besides the main course. Harbajan was speaking about many things to Ashok Kumar and sometimes to Arjun when Ashok Kumar also spoke to him while Arjun remained reticent   most of the times. The man from Punjab said good opinion about the food, after finishing which, Ashok Kumar, Arjun and Harbajan Singh went to wash their hands. They moved to the wash basin amid other passengers many of whom had finished eating. There were couples, lovers, friends and relatives among the passengers. Couples and lovers seemed to be in a loving mood as they said sweet nothings to each other. Anybody would desire his or her lover to be with him or her during a journey. Such a feeling was there in the minds of Ashok Kumar, Arjun and Harbajan Singh as Ashok Kumar thought about his life with Kaveri that he had loved his wife so much. Remembrances of his bygone years with Kaveri came to his mind while Arjun was thinking about Pooja when he saw the couples loving each other and the uxorious Harbajan Singh too was thinking about his sweetheart who is in Punjab. They were realizing that love is a special thing; what feeling does it bring to our minds beggars description. They laved their hands and came back to their seats as many of the passengers who seemed to be aristocratic and rich were coming to wash their hands.

Arjun, Ashok kumar and Harbajan Singh sat in their seats cosily. This time Arjun asked his father to sit near the porthole. Arjun sat in between Ashok Kumar and Harbajan Singh. Harbajan Singh smiled to Arjun in a more friendly way and Arjun smiled to him back with the same vigour.

"Do you like visiting Punjab?" Harbajan Singh asked Arjun after sometime.

"Yes, certainly," Arjun replied with enthusiasm.

"What do you know about Punjab?" The Sikh man asked further.

"Several things," Arjun said smiling.

"Like what?"

"There exists a religion solely for the people of Punjab. Then I have learned about Gyani Zail Singh and Guru Nanak. Then, I like cricketers like Yuvraj Singh, Harbajan Singh, Navajyoth Singh Sidhu and Bollywood stars like Chandrachood Singh and Dara Singh," Arjun talked, stopping at certain points and then resuming.

Harbajan Singh felt merry to hear Arjun speaking about his native land and he liked the adolescent very much when Ashok Kumar turned to them occasionally from the direction of the porthole. Many of the passengers talked among themselves while many others did not talk much and majority of those who were travelling alone seldom talked. There were passengers from different countries, congregated under a roof.

The passengers turned to the back side of the plane suddenly, hearing a loud scream. A little girl was crying and her parents are trying to console her. She was crying because she saw a dreadful dream in which she saw some aliens coming to attack her. All the passengers who heard the yell were relieved that there was nothing to worry about and so, not everyone went to see her but many. There were Ashok Kumar, Arjun and Harbajan Singh among those who went to see the child. The girl of may be seven years of age has ceased crying by now as others asked her what she saw in the dream, the girl describing to them that three extraterrestrials were coming to her to catch her. Those who met together there, consoled her saying to her that she has nothing to be perturbed about, and it was only a dream that she saw. An airhostess gave her sweets while other airhostesses tried to gladden her as they had come to her, hearing the cry. A passenger opined that children are always watching cartoons in which extraterrestrials are the main characters. The girl was voyaging along with her parents and she had fallen asleep about half an hour ago.

Later, the passengers came back to their seats. Arjun sat where he sat earlier and so did Ashok Kumar and Harbajan Singh and the aeroplane flew above the Arabian sea as Arjun and Ashok Kumar knew, they are flying above the sea though they could see nothing through the porthole as darkness had pervaded everywhere outside the plane. But later, as the plane moved further, they could see lights as the plane is above a city of an Arabian country. They were not able to know which city it was. Anyway, Arjun and Ashok Kumar knew that the journey is going to end very soon. They had gained knowledge of the pleasure of flying in a plane over time which was unfamiliar to them and they had realized that the pleasure of journey in a plane is far beyond the pleasure of journey in a car or train.

Later, an airhostess asked the passengers to tie their seatbelts as the plane was going to land and all the passengers fastened their seatbelts when Arjun and Ashok Kumar felt uneasy whether the difficulty they had earlier during the take off would again come to them during the plane's landing. Harbajan Singh, who had a turban on his head, patted on it as it seemed he wanted to touch the top of his head. The male Sikhs never in their life, cut their hair. The passengers experienced the difficulty as the plane landed like what they experienced on the take off when the plane rose at the beginning of its trip.

The plane has reached the city of Doha, which is the capital of Qatar; there were lights all over the city and the airport. The plane put down on the runway of Doha International Airport which is one of the largest airports in the world, while Ashok Kumar and Arjun were full of desire to see Qatar that they had heard about Qatar from Ashok Kumar's eldest brother, his family and others and they knew, Qatar is one of the wealthiest countries in the world as petrol has brought riches into this country like other Arabian countries.

The plane stopped altogether after running on the runway and all the passengers are now in a mood to not to fly after a pleasant journey as they now are desirous to come out of the plane. They untied their seatbelts and stood up from their seats and they were in a relaxed mood. All the passengers were looking around to see others. There were seven or eight people besides Ashok Kumar and Arjun who were flying in an aeroplane for the first time. Passengers walked to the door of the plane where airhostesses stood near the doorway, smiling as if saying that the passengers should come again. The passengers came out of the plane through the ladder of the plane to the ground.

All the travellers walked to the airport building. Many of them are coming to Qatar for the first time. Arjun and Ashok Kumar felt that the feeling is unlike watching on

YouTube when one sees a foreign country directly, especially for those coming from countries like India, Sri Lanka and Pakistan. There were people gathered in the airport terminal to greet the passengers on arrival who were their relatives, friends and the like among whom there were Ashok Kumar's eldest brother and his family who have come to receive them. Arjun, Ashok Kumar and Harbajan Singh entered the airport building after ten or eleven people, who went before them.

CHAPTER 5

After waiting for about forty five minutes, Ashok Kumar's eldest brother Vishal and his family could meet Ashok Kumar and Arjun when they came out to them after they completed the procedures and possessed their luggage. Vishal had come with his wife and three children. As Ashok Kumar and Arjun came near to them they smiled with affection to them and Ashok Kumar and Arjun smiled to them back lovingly. Both the father and the son came outside the terminal, the father pushing the trolley containing their luggage. Vishal, his wife and three children came to them. Vishal asked his brother and nephew how the journey was to which Ashok Kumar responded that it was very fine when Arjun too said that it was fantastic. They knew that Arjun and Ashok Kumar are for the first time travelling in a plane. The wife and children of Vishal were seen talking to Arjun and Ashok Kumar something or the other. The youngest boy of three boys of Vishal was the age of Arjun.

Harbajan Singh too was with Ashok Kumar and Arjun, pushing trolley. Ashok Kumar introduced him to Vishal and his family. Harbajan Singh talked to them about where he lived and where he is employed as Vishal too said to him about his whereabouts and after sometime a friend of Harbajan Singh came to him and picked him who too talked to all of them. He too was a Sikh man. Later, both men from Punjab left them and Ashok Kumar, Arjun, Vishal and others tramped to where vehicles had been parked. All of them ascended the SUV which Vishal owned after placing the bags in the dickey, and after that, the vehicle moved, which was driven by Karan, the eldest son of Vishal. The SUV moved in between other vehicles. Ashok kumar was seated in the front seat, Vishal, his wife and Vishal's second son in the middle and the others in the back seat as it was a big SUV in which more than five travellers could travel.

The SUV was heading towards Vishal's house, which was in the capital city itself when Arjun and Ashok Kumar looked outside through the glass and saw the sights in Doha city which as they were seeing for the first time, they were much impressed. They thought, it is very much like what they saw on YouTube apart from the fact that the feeling when one discerns it directly is different. They could see gorgeous shops all along the roadside which had a uniformity and they could see people from different countries assembled all over the area. The SUV ran in a moderate speed inside which Ashok Kumar, Vishal and others did not talk much apart from speaking occasionally. The city was as if adorned by lights, in the night.

They reached the destined spot after a running of about half an hour. That was an area where residences could be seen everywhere where there were few shops. Vishal lived in a villa for rent near which there were five villas that was given for rent to families. Vishal, Ashok Kumar and others descended from the SUV after Vishal's eldest son parked it in a shed that was proximate to their house and they went to their house, which was a two storeyed one above which another family lived who also were from India.

It was a beautiful house with three bedrooms each in two storeys. Ashok Kumar and Arjun sat in the guest room with others as they talked something to their relatives, and later, they went to other rooms just to perceive the rooms. Vishal was an engineer and he was somewhat rich. The rooms were neat and compactly arranged. Later, Ashok Kumar and Arjun were called for supper and they were served with Kubboose, prawns curry and crab fry after which there were ice cream and pudding as desserts. They dined with Vishal and his children when Vishal's wife, Rekha brought the things they wanted.

After dinner, Vishal said that they would be going to explore the Doha city the next day as he said he has taken leave from his office for three days and he requested Ashok Kumar and Arjun to slumber with his sons together in their beds. When it turned to be 10 o'clock, Arjun and Ashok Kumar went to sleep after watching television for sometime in which they saw many channels of different countries more than that they saw in India. Arjun lay with Karan and Ashok Kumar lay with Ajay and Akshay as they were the other two sons of Vishal. They didn't talk much but considered thoughtfully on several things of which the main subject was kaveri. Arjun and Ashok Kumar cried in their minds remembering about Kaveri. It has become many days since she departed from this life and they were sorrowful to not to see her for days.

The next day, Ashok Kumar and Arjun woke early when all the others too woke later. Arjun peered outside through the window when it was four thirty at first light and he felt that the atmosphere is somewhat the same as the atmosphere when he was in India. He remained there for a long time before going to the bathroom to brush his teeth and all and it was when Karan called him, he realized that he has been positioned near the window for a long time.

"Arjun, how is morning here?" Karan asked him smiling, seeing him looking outside through the casement.

"Oh, it is very nice," Arjun responded.

"Are you going to the bathroom first or may I go?" Karan asked him as there was a bathroom attached to the room.

"You go first," Arjun answered politely.

"Okay then," saying thus Karan opened the door of the bathroom and entered it.

Later, after coming from the bathroom, Arjun came to the guest room and he saw Karan and all others assembled there as it seemed all of them were waiting for him and when they saw him they gave him a smile.

"Come Arjun, we can have breakfast. I think you have bathed," Vishal said to Arjun smilingly, thinking Arjun must have bathed because of him coming late.

After breakfast, Vishal, Ashok Kumar and others came out of the house after about an hour and Vishal locked the door of the house and they walked to the proximity of their vehicle to the car shed and they ascended it unhurriedly. The time is ten and five. This time, it was Vishal who drove the SUV and Ashok Kumar sat in the front seat near Vishal and others in the middle seat and in the back seat. The SUV moved to the front as it was positioned thus to take to the front directly, the previous day. The vehicle moved, and later, it moved through the main road in the city of Doha.

"We shall go to the zoo today. Then we can go to parks, corniche and the likes," Vishal said to Ashok Kumar, looking at others also to the back, while driving.

"Yeah, how far is the zoo from here?" Ashok Kumar asked Vishal.

"We can reach there within fifty minutes," Vishal said looking straight.

Ashok Kumar shook his head as others were listening to them without speaking anything. Arjun sat in the middle seat near the left window behind his father and looked at things outside and he felt that the city is very different from the Indian cities that it is maintained very tidily and beautifully. When Vishal and his family viewed the sights as something they are accustomed to, Ashok Kumar and Arjun were watching the sights as something new to them. The city was crowded with people from all over the world who were affluent and there were people who were not rich among them and there were a lot of people who were good looking and elevated among whom there were people who were not that good looking. On the road, there were a number of cars and other vehicles running along to both sides, and on the whole, they brought a figure of richness to the eyes of a spectator. All of the shops were splendent unlike the shops in Indian cities, where not every shop is extravagant, but some. Ashok Kumar, Arjun and others saw the shops filled with customers. There were huge buildings on both sides of the road which were hotels, flats, offices and the like and there were restaurants, jewellery shops, textile shops, malls and so on along the roadside.

The SUV ran aiming the zoo along the road which after passing the city ran in between residential areas and deserts when Arjun and Ashok Kumar was fascinated by the sights outside the city. They were thrilled to travel through deserts. They looked at the vast deserts with delight, where there was no much human inhabitation. They saw many other vehicles passing by them who may be, as they thought, going to the zoo like them. As they journeyed further, an open jeep went past them, in which there were five youngsters, shouting and laughing boisterously, looking at other passengers; they were dressed freakishly and one could make out, they are drunk by the way they behaved. Arjun, Ashok Kumar and others watched them with curiosity that they used to see such youngsters when they visited tourist spots. Arjun remembered his such playful schoolmates who behaved like this when teachers are not around.

Ashok Kumar, Vishal and others reached the zoo on 11 o' clock. There were tourists all over the area many of whom standing in a queue to take tickets to enter the zoo. Vishal parked the SUV where parking was allowed and all of them descended from the SUV and stood near it, looking around to see the sights there of the portal of the zoo and its surroundings. There was a big crowd over there composed of adults and young ones who were in a jolly mood, they looked around to see other human beings like them. Later, Ashok Kumar, Vishal and others stood in the line of persons awaiting their turn. After taking tickets, they entered the zoo. The zoo was a very big one and there were a lot of people inside it who spent a lot of time there, coming with families, comrades and relatives. There were almost all the animals and birds there, which one could see in forests, caged and preserved in big areas such as lions, tigers and rhinoceros. Reptiles like crocodiles and semi aquatic mammals like hippopotamus are kept in areas with pools.

Vishal, Ashok Kumar and others perambulated inside the zoo observing beasts and our feathered friends, identifying each creature. There were boards near each cage, written in detail about the enclosed animals and birds which the visitors read with interest and some of them were seen to be giving something for them to eat. Arjun and Ashok Kumar had visited zoos in India and they realized that there are more animals and birds in this zoo than in the zoos there. All of them strolled to see every animal and bird. Later, they saw animals such as zebra and giraffes, which were kept in large areas to where the visitors can see only from a distance.

By 3'o clock, they came out of the zoo. They thought about eating something as they had postponed to do it after coming out of the zoo; they had bought some snacks and cool drinks before that, that they did not feel much hunger. Vishal, Ashok Kumar and others dined out at a restaurant nearby, and later, they went home.

CHAPTER 6

Three days passed. Ashok Kumar, Vishal and others went to different places in Qatar and after Vishal's leave expired, he went to his work place and so did his three sons as they went to their educational institutions. Ashok Kumar and Arjun remained with Vishal's wife in the residence. They whiled away the time there till noon, watching television and reading books and after that Vishal's wife, Rekha served them luncheon which was mutton biriyani and Ashok kumar and Arjun dined the tasty Indian dish. Afterwards, they decided to go to Doha city unaccompanied by Vishal and his family and they said to Rekha about it and she responded positively to it allowing them to go. Later, they set out from the house, hired a taxi as Vishal had taken his vehicle with him to his office. They went to Doha city.

As the taxi moved, Arjun and Ashok Kumar watched the sights outside, which had become familiar to them by travelling for three days. The driver was a middle aged man from Philippines who asked Ashok Kumar, who was sitting on the front seat, about his whereabouts in English as he spoke good English and Ashok Kumar replied telling him that he was from India and other things. The man who introduced himself as Javad seemed to be a very nice man whose conduct was good. He asked Arjun his name and in which standard he studied. The car moved as they talked to each other.

The car ran through the city and Ashok Kumar requested the driver to stop the car when it reached near a mall. They could read the name of the mall which was written in big letters on its front and there were bags of people gathered in its tract many of whom carried bags after doing their shopping and there could be seen a number of vehicles coming from and going to the mall. There were people in great numbers as it seemed something special was going to occur there. Ashok Kumar and Arjun descended from the taxi and walked to the mall after giving the driver his due. The mall was very big and it had five storeys which consisted of a lot of shops of apparels, jewellery, watches and the likes.

Arjun and Ashok Kumar legged it a little further and entered the mall along with those coming to the mall in that afternoon. It was very large to see from the inside where there was an empty space in the middle, and escalators connecting each floor, where there were shops and footways on the three sides of the mall contrary to the forepart which faced the road. There were tiny shops on the ground floor's empty space and the pathways of other storeys. Arjun and Ashok Kumar could make out that any one of the celebrities is coming there that afternoon, from the number of people assembled there, that they thought any new shop must be going to be inaugurated by the star. The people seemed to be waiting eagerly for that celebrated person to come, from their body languages. Ashok Kumar and Arjun looked around to see the particular shop which is going to be inaugurated and they found it, being a jewellery shop on the first floor as they saw people thronged there.

"Dad, shall we go there?" Arjun asked Ashok Kumar intending to go to the jewellery shop.

They had not spoken about the inauguration, but, both of them knew that the other has made it out.

"Yeah, come. Let us go there," Ashok Kumar said.

Ashok Kumar and Arjun moved to the first floor by the escalator and on reaching there they plodded to the shop, which was going to be inaugurated, amid the people who were there in great numbers. They could know the famous person who was coming there for inauguration, from the mouths of those gathered there and they could also know that he would be coming at any time. It was Bobbey Deol, the young sensation of Bollywood, who is coming for inauguration to that mall who was supposed to come on 3o' clock. It has become three thirty and people are looking for his arrival at any time.

A little later, the body languages of the people said that Bobbey Deol has arrived that all of them gaped at the car in which he is coming when those who were nearby the car ran into it to see the star. Bobbey Deol descended from the car when the crowd rushed to him. It was the police officers who controlled the crowd when people tried to touch him and embrace him and they helped him to go to the mall amongst the people. People from all over came running to see the film star and there occurred a traffic block on the roads and one could see all the passengers looking at the mall from the vehicles. Anyway, the 'tinsel star' got in to the mall and he walked to the jewellery shop to inaugurate it for which he took some time. Arjun and Ashok Kumar too wanted to touch and hold the star as they too rushed to him like others.

Bobbey Deol inaugurated the shop by cutting a long piece of cloth by scissors when all the people looked at him with great amazement as they thought he is really handsome like the hero, they see in films, they expressed great admiration for the star that he was more proficient than other actors in the world. Everybody was provided with tea and snacks by the owners of the shop after the inauguration and Bobbey Deol chatted with the owners and later he decided to go back. It was difficult to go out through that rush but the police officers led him forward through the gap among the multitude like they earlier brought him to the shop that they held back the movements of the people towards the star and made way for the actor to go and after sometime the star reached his car and he ascended it and disappeared later, when the crowd looked at the car with a feeling of losing something, dearly loved.

Ashok Kumar and Arjun watched the car till it was lost to view from their sights standing in the first floor of the mall near the glass at the forepart of the building, through which they could see things outside the mall. The number of the people decreased gradually as the film star quitted. After half an hour, both of them could walk easily inside the mall, they perambulated inside it for some time and later, they entered a supermarket inside the mall. They had to buy something or the other to take to India when they go to India after days, to give them to their relatives, friends and all. They looked for toys, packed food items and the like. There was everything available in that supermarket from pencils to big toys. Ashok Kumar and Arjun bought ten items of things within one hour and they came back from the supermarket after paying for those and they carried the bags in their hands as they were not many. They thought to buy other things in the coming days.

Then, they decided to have dinner and Ashok Kumar spoke to his brother by his mobile phone that they would be coming home after dining and he and Arjun looked for a restaurant inside the mall. Later, they found a dining area on the fourth floor and they entered it.

"What would you like to have?" Ashok Kumar asked Arjun after they sat in cushioned chairs on both sides of a table which was   placed almost in the middle of the hall.

"Shall we eat fried chicken?" Arjun asked Ashok Kumar in a way that he thought that his father would like his suggestion.

"Yeah, let us have it," Ashok Kumar said.

He ordered a full Kentucky fried chicken for both of them when a waiter came to them and he looked at Arjun when the waiter   queried him what they would like to drink. Arjun looked at Ashok Kumar and said that he would like Pepsi, Ashok kumar ordered the waiter to bring two cans of Pepsi along with the fried chicken.

The waiter brought the food after sometime and both father and son set about eating it when abruptly Ashok Kumar saw a friend of him, coming to him smilingly. It was his former classmate in the college, Imran, who saw him when he was passing by. Both friends are meeting after years, yet, they didn't have any difficulty in recognizing each other as both of them have not altered much. Imran was alone and he pulled a seat near the table and sat on it after shaking hands with Ashok kumar and asking him whether he identified him or not.

"Are you working here?" Imran asked Ashok Kumar still beaming.

"No, I came here for only one week to visit my brother," Ashok Kumar replied, smiling to him.

"This is your son?" Imran asked Ashok Kumar, looking at Arjun too.

"Yes, he is my only son," Ashok Kumar replied, looking affectionately at his son.

Imran smiled to Arjun and Arjun smiled to him back. Ashok Kumar introduced Imran to Arjun that he was a classmate of him when he studied for postgraduate course in English. Ashok Kumar and Imran conversed to each other for some time, Imran partaking the fried chicken with them as Ashok Kumar asked him to do so. Ashok Kumar told him about the death of his wife and all, and Imran felt pity for the father and the son. After fifteen minutes, Imran said to Ashok Kumar that he is retiring and they can meet later, after they had talked about almost all the matters, they had to talk about and Imran shook hands with Ashok Kumar and Arjun, smilingly and left.

Later, Ashok Kumar and Arjun finished eating, they stood up and went to wash their hands. There were people almost in every seat and there were adults and children walking in between the tables, and some of them ordering food and many going to wash their hands like Arjun and Ashok Kumar. People looked around to see others. Ashok Kumar and Arjun washed their hands and came out of the dining area. They perambulated further inside the mall to see whatever is there inside the mall and they found a number of shops which were of fabrics, watches and the like. They had no much time to do further shopping or to visit many shops, so, they made up their minds to pass some time in an area where there were equipments for children to play like car driving, table tennis, shooting, etc. and they entered such an area. There were children and adults playing games like bowling and table tennis. Ashok Kumar and Arjun tried some of the sports for half an hour like others and they came out of the area afterwards and walked to the escalator and descended through it to the ground floor. On reaching the ground floor they bought two ice creams for themselves and after having which they quitted the gorgeous mall.

Later, they walked through the pavement, watching the sights in the city and when a taxi passed by Ashok Kumar showed his hand to the driver for him to stop it and he and Arjun ascended the taxi after the driver stopped it. The car moved to Vishal's house as Ashok Kumar had informed the driver the exact destination as there was a petrol pump near Vishal's house, the name of which he had mentioned to the driver.

CHAPTER 7

The next day, Ashok Kumar and Arjun rose at 7o' clock in the morning. This time, they had slept together as Vishal's three sons slept together in the other room. Arjun went to bathe first and Ashok Kumar read a novel, which he got from that chamber, which was 'The Grand Babylon Hotel' written by Arnold Bennett and when Arjun came back from the bathroom, he went to it to bathe. Arjun put on his dresses, which was a brown tee-shirt with something written on them and a pair of blue jeans and after that he looked at the novel, which was placed on the bed by Ashok Kumar, he found the novel being well written and having a good narrative by reading the summary printed on the back cover of the novel. When Ashok Kumar came back from the bathroom, they went to the guestroom after Ashok Kumar put on his apparels and they saw there, Vishal and his three sons. When Ashok Kumar and Arjun entered the room, all of them smiled to them and Vishal requested them to sit.

After breakfast, Ashok Kumar and Arjun determined to go out after Vishal and his sons went out and they set out to the city after mentioning Vishal's wife, Rekha about it. They hired a taxi and went to the city. Ashok Kumar thought of going to the seacoast this time and he told Arjun about it. The driver was a youngster from Pakistan who enquired Ashok Kumar, where he hailed from and other things and Ashok Kumar too talked to him, whose name was Shoaib. Arjun too talked to him. The driver stopped the vehicle when the car reached near the corniche and Ashok Kumar and Arjun alighted from the car and Ashok Kumar paid the driver.

Ashok kumar and Arjun sat on the sands looking at the vast sea among a lot of others who have come with their family, friends and relatives, and they talked to each other about several things with abounding affection expressed to each other. When one loves inside his or her mind, he or she likes to show it outwards, otherwise, not. Ashok Kumar loved his only son than anyone else in this world that he was not able to live without him for a moment and Arjun too loved his father, the same way his father loved him. Being in the seashore with someone, one loves is a different feeling that Ashok Kumar and Arjun experienced that emotion as they sat cheek by jowl for long on the sands. Though they talked to each other, they remained silent most of the times. They could see mortals, coming, going and remaining there, from where they sat. Later, they walked here and there among the people.

Ashok kumar and Arjun walked along the road after they came back from the corniche to hire a taxi that they had decided to go back to Vishal's house before lunch as Vishal's wife had asked them to come in the noon. Arjun saw a man looking at him without taking eyes, as he turned to his left; he could not make out what the matter was. Ashok Kumar too discerned the man, looking constantly at Arjun and he too wanted to know, what the matter was. As the man saw Ashok kumar and Arjun looking at him, he stopped staring at them and they thought, the man must have taken them wrongly as somebody, he knew.

The man, Paresh could not believe his eyes that whom he searched for years is appeared before his eyes. All these years, he was searching for his lost child who had been vanished eight years ago and now, he has found him out. There was no limit to his happiness that he became sure that his son is alive as he was not sure even that he is in existence. Paresh had loved his son that much that he was not able to stand the grief of losing his only son who was lost when he was five years old during a visit to the Taj Mahal at Agra, India. When Paresh spent time inside the Taj with his wife and son, their son Deepak went away from them to other people as his parents failed to notice that for some time. By the time they thought about Deepak after taking pleasure in the marvellous sculptures inside Taj Mahal, he had been lost in the crowd. Paresh and his wife Divya scoured and scoured everywhere but without any result. They did whatever they could, including giving petition in the nearby police station and since then, the unfortunate parents are searching everywhere for their child.

Paresh found that the boy is his offspring as he greatly resembles Deepak and Deepak would have become of his age if he lived now. From these reasons, Paresh made certain that Arjun is his son and the man with him must have got him from somewhere. Arjun looked exactly like Deepak that Paresh was not dubious that he may not be his son.

Paresh turned to his back side when Arjun and Ashok Kumar looked at him and then he viewed them again when they moved forward, he decided to follow them and he walked behind them, three or four metres away.

His mind was saying: "My son, my son! How I yearned to see you all these years! Where were you, my son?"

Ashok Kumar and Arjun didn't see the man though they looked all round to see him that whenever they looked to their back side, Paresh turned about to his back side, they not to see him. Ashok Kumar showed his hand to a taxi driver and the taxi stopped beside them and as they got into it, Paresh too hired a taxi and asked the driver to follow it. The car, in which Arjun and Ashok Kumar travelled, moved forward when the car, in which Paresh was travelling, pursued it with the same speed as the other. Paresh feared that if he claimed that the boy is his son, the man with him might not like it as it might be he who fostered him.

The taxi stopped in front of Vishal's house and both Ashok Kumar and Arjun descended from the car and they went to the house after paying the driver when the taxi, in which Paresh travelled, stopped on the other side of the road as Vishal's house was on the roadside. Paresh too got down from the car and paid the driver. Then, he remained there looking at Vishal's house for sometime after the driver withdrew. Arjun and Ashok Kumar was not to be seen from there even if they may be outside the house, because of the wall around the house that Paresh tried to see them coming near to the house.

Paresh tried to see Arjun in any manner whatever, but, he couldn't see him from outside the house, so, he returned to the city after staying there for one hour, walking here and there. When he reached the city, he went to a delicatessen and ate lunch. He was reflecting on Arjun all the time that he felt to run to him, he took liquor to get relieved as he had begun to drink from the day he lost Deepak. He had loved Deepak intensively and he still remembers Deepak loving him back so much. Paresh was very gleeful though he did not get his son back, that he knew that his son is alive and he saw him.

Later, Paresh decided to go home and see his wife, who too was waiting for the past eight years, her son to return. She was perusing a magazine, sitting in the portico when Paresh opened the gate of his abode after he descended from a taxi and gave money to the driver; Paresh approached his wife with a rapturous countenance that his wife Divya felt something unusual has happened. She doubted, may be it was because he might have found their son as she had been accustomed to seeing her husband gloomy all the time after his son's loss. She too was not in a different condition all these years.

"Divya...I saw Deepak!" Paresh said to her in one breath with wonder in his eyes.

"Really?" Divya couldn't believe what he said.

"Where did you find him?" Divya asked before Paresh said anything.

Paresh narrated everything to her as she stood wonderstruck. After hearing everything, Divya did not utter anything for some time, later, she said to her husband that they have to assure themselves that the boy is theirs, she was very happy to hear that her son has been found out. Paresh and Divya sat there in the portico, thinking what to do next.

*   *   *   *   *

Inside Vishal's house, Arjun was deliberating about the man whom he met that day, sitting in the bed, where he slept last night. He thought, what was in his eyes? Love, wonder or what? Why did he stare at him? The man seemed to be of his father's age, may be around forty five. Arjun surmised that the man must have thought about him to be his son that the way he looked at him seemed to be so, he felt pity for the man, that he must have lost his son. Arjun and Ashok Kumar had seen the man meandering outside the house for about an hour.

Arjun looked again to where he saw the man but couldn't see him. He looked time and again as time went by, but the man did not come, and later, he watched television in which he saw the movie, 'Phool aur Kante' as he inserted its video cassette into the VCR. He had seen the film twice and he knew the story, it being about a father longing for the love of his son, who hates his father. Arjun sympathized with that man, who followed them, when he saw the movie, that he wished to go to that man and console him. Arjun had talked to his father about that man and his father too talked to him about the man empathetically.

Time passed. This time Vishal's wife prepared supper early and everybody in that house dined when it was only 8o' clock. They ate Kubboos and chicken fry to which there was prawns curry to pour to the Kubboos which was having a very pleasant flavour and Ashok Kumar did not forget to praise Vishal's wife that she made it very tastily. After the supper, Vishal, Ashok Kumar and others went to bed soon. Only Ashok Kumar and Arjun thought about Paresh as others had neither seen him nor known about him.

Ashok Kumar and Arjun lay in the same room and as it was early, they did not become drowsy and they spent time without sleeping. Ashok Kumar lay on the bed facing upwards tying his hands under his head while Arjun lay sideways facing Ashok Kumar.

*   *   *   *   *

At the same time, Paresh and his wife dined supper, they were hopeful to know their son is alive after years, but the fact that there is possibility, the boy to be not their son saddened both of them and they were in a nervous condition emerged out of the thought that the adolescent may or may not be their son. After dinner, both of them went to bed, and later, Divya told her husband that they should assure themselves that whether the boy is their son or not by asking the man, who was seen with him. They passed time with the intention to go and see the man the next day, and they fell to sleep later.

CHAPTER 8

There is only two days left for Ashok Kumar and Arjun to return to India and they thought about going to the city this day too after they got up from the bed, the next morning. After the first meal of the day, vishal, his family, Ashok Kumar and Arjun decided to go out as they all were free, it being a holiday. They all set out when it was nine thirty in Vishal's SUV to Doha city, all of them were in a jolly mood that it is always fun to travel in group rather than going alone. The vehicle moved to Doha city as Vishal steered it when some of the passengers talked this and that and some others did not talk much.

Vishal, Ashok Kumar and others walked on foot in the city after they reached the city and descended from the SUV and parked it. Arjun was in good company with Vishal's three sons and they chatted among themselves as they moved and Ashok Kumar talked to Vishal something or the other while Vishal's wife lacked a good company as there wasn't a female among them for her to be friendly with, but she talked to her husband and others, which seemed, it was not a problem to her. All of them walked along the road on the side of which, there were a lot of shops to which they looked from time to time as if they intended to buy something from there.

There were a good deal of people walking with them who might have come for shopping and other purposes, and inside each shop, there were a lot of people, making it time-consuming to buy anything from there. When Ashok Kumar, Vishal and others reached near an apparel shop, they stopped walking as Vishal said to others that he wishes to buy some dresses for Ashok kumar and Arjun.

All of them entered the shop, which was big and which sold apparels for men only. At first, Vishal decided to buy dresses for Arjun and then to Ashok Kumar and he asked one of the salesmen to show readymade dresses suitable for boys of his age to which the salesman requested them to go to the first floor as it was a two storeyed building and dresses for boys of his age were available there as on the ground floor, readymade dresses for adults were available. Ashok Kumar, Vishal and others ascended to the first floor by the stairway and they all kept in view, the salesman showing Arjun, different apparels. All of them joined Arjun in selecting the dresses that they suggested Arjun as, this would be nice for him and that would be nice for him.

After sometime, Arjun picked one shirt, one tee-shirt, a pair of jeans and a pair of pants for himself, and later, they descended to the ground floor to buy shirts and pants for Ashok Kumar; Ashok Kumar looked for pants and shirts of his choice among the large variety of dresses displayed for men, he looked for plain and check shirts and dark colour pants. Arjun showed him a check shirt of yellow and black colours and Ashok Kumar selected that for himself, and later, he bought one more shirt and two pairs of trousers. Arjun too had bought a check shirt among others. Later, Vishal paid the bill as he had bought the dresses as a present to his younger brother and nephew.

Ashok kumar, Vishal and others came out of the shop, and then, they proceeded near to their vehicle. Ashok Kumar placed the bags in the SUV'S dickey and Vishal locked it, and then, they walked some distance to a nearby restaurant; they entered the restaurant which was somewhat big and they seated themselves on the chairs around two tables after they washed their hands. Vishal ordered some seafood for everybody after seeking others' opinions, which were crab roast and prawns fry along with some rice for all. It was an Indian restaurant serving seafood and meat. After dining, they came out of the restaurant and walked to where their vehicle was. It was early that they ate the food. Later, they ascended the SUV and it rode to a nearby park, where people were less as it was noon.

Vishal, Ashok Kumar and others gained access to the park. It was a beautiful park with a lot of plants, bearing beautiful flowers and a lot of trees on its borders. There was a large area amid plants and trees for people to walk on where there was lawns of superior fibres and there were seats for the visitors to sit on amidst plants carrying beautiful flowers and florets which were planted artistically and preserved carefully. Ashok Kumar, Arjun and others sat on the benches which were there in plenty, where visitors walked. There was breeze all over the public garden as it was a pleasant experience to have a whale of a time in the noon. There were children running around over there, who were controlled by elders. There were people from different countries, among whom Ashok kumar and others saw so many Indians. Vishal, Ashok Kumar and others just sat on the benches without perambulating here and there. Later, they went back to their house.

Ashok Kumar and Arjun saw the man, who followed them yesterday, standing in front of Vishal's house with a woman, when they reached there. Arjun and Ashok Kumar surmised what the matter was, that they might have come to know, if Arjun was their son and both of them felt sympathy for the couple, as they thought, the woman may be the man's wife. Vishal and others too saw the man and woman, whom they could not recognize, standing in front of their gate and everybody descended from the SUV after Vishal parking it in the car shed.

Vishal, Ashok Kumar and others approached the man and woman, who were waiting there for a long time and all of them looked at the couple in a manner, they wanting to know, who they were. The man and woman smiled at them amicably when Vishal asked them who they were and what they wanted.

"I am Paresh and this is my wife, Divya," The middle aged man said, looking at Vishal.

"Where are you from?" Vishal asked him.

"We are from Maharashtra, India," the man continued.

Everybody had thought on them beforehand that they may be from India and sometimes from Maharashtra from their appearances.

"I want to talk to you," Paresh said after a pause, looking at Ashok Kumar and then to Arjun.

"Then, come inside the house," Vishal said to him, inviting him to his house.

Paresh and Divya entered the house along with others and they sat on the chairs in the portico. Arjun looked fixedly at both of them and he stood beside his father. Paresh began to speak in a low voice that he feared what he was going to tell them would not be liked by them as, Vishal and others looked at him inquisitively that they had no idea what the man is going to say.

"I am going to talk about your son," Paresh looked at Ashok Kumar and said.

"Please say," Ashok Kumar said to him friendly.

"That, I suspect him to be my son," Paresh spoke to Ashok Kumar hesitatingly.

Ashok Kumar and Arjun had expected him saying so while others could not make it out before.

"How can it be possible?" Ashok Kumar asked Paresh with a changed countenance which showed, he didn't like the statement.

Paresh did not speak for some time. He looked at Ashok Kumar as if he said, what should not have said.

"I mean, that I suspect him to be my lost child," he said later.

"This boy very much takes after our lost child," Divya, who did not speak anything till then, said looking at Arjun and then at Ashok Kumar.

"But, he is my son," Ashok Kumar said.

"We have come here to know the truth as my husband saw him at the city, yesterday,"

"Where did you lose him?" Vishal asked Divya.

Divya narrated to them what happened to their son. Everybody listened to her eagerly.

"But, Arjun is my son. You are mistaken," Ashok Kumar said to Divya sympathetically.

Divya said nothing. She just smiled looking affectionately at Arjun. She was almost convinced that Arjun was not her son when Paresh was not ready to believe Ashok Kumar.

Paresh did not speak anything, but, in his mind, he was sure that Arjun is his son and he decided to pursue him and make him, his own. Later, Vishal's wife brought them apple juices with some snacks after they sat in the guestroom as per the invitation of Vishal.

Paresh and Divya asked Arjun several things about him to which Arjun answered them politely; both Paresh and Divya remained there for some more time and they went back to their house afterwards after taking leave of Ashok Kumar, Arjun and others. Everybody had acquitted themselves to them sympathetically, realizing how painful it would be to lose one's offspring for years, they had asked them many things about their son, Deepak including the procedures they done to find him.

Paresh drove the car in which he and Divya came as Divya looked outside with tears in her eyes; Paresh was not that sad that he believed firmly that Arjun is his son. They did not talk for sometime but later Ashok Kumar began a conversation.

"What do you think Divya, isn't it Deepak?"

"I have no much hope. I don't think, they are lying," Divya said in a pathetic tone.

"But, I think, they are prevaricating," Paresh enunciated.

Divya did not speak. She knew, Paresh would say like that, knowing his character. They talked as the car moved, and later, they went to the beach, spent time there. Paresh and Divya looked at children and adults that how lucky they were to live with their parents and children. They sat on the sands as Divya seemed to be with a feeling of loss and Paresh seemed to be with a feeling that he has got back something valuable. After about forty five minutes, they got up to go back and they approached their car, which was parked nearby and ascended it promptly and after sometime, the car ran amidst other vehicles.

*   *   *   *   *

Arjun looked at Ashok Kumar a little suspiciously when they went to bed and he asked: "Dad, is there any truth in that man's words?" he had postponed asking his father thus to a later occasion when others are not around.

"No my son, you are my son surely. Why should you worry if others say anything?" Ashok Kumar looked at Arjun affectionately when he said so.

"Dad, I cannot bear it, if you are not my father," Arjun said lovingly.

"Believe me Arjun, you ask any of our relatives, if you doubt," Ashok Kumar's words soothed Arjun. He embraced his father as they lay on the bed.

Both father and son remained in that position for long. Outside the house, it was hot and air condition was working in the room. There were fleets of vehicles passing by on the road and people walking and there appeared aeroplanes in the sky below which birds of a feather flocked together. Arjun and Ashok Kumar fell asleep later when the clock rang ten in the night.

CHAPTER 9

A week elapsed from the day Arjun and Ashok Kumar   landed in Qatar. Now, they are leaving Qatar and returns to India. The flight is at 4 o' clock in the afternoon and they are packing their luggage in the morning at 7 o' clock before having breakfast to which Vishal and his sons joined and Rekha was busy preparing breakfast for them. Vishal and his sons had taken leave that day to bid them farewell. Ajay,

Akshay, Karan and Vishal lent Ashok kumar and Arjun a helping hand to pack their things, which they took to India with them like toys, packed food items and dresses. Later, they ate breakfast together and after that, they resumed packing.

After lunch, everybody came out of their house and Vishal locked the door from outside and all of them walked to the car shed; the SUV came out of the outhouse after everyone of them ascended it and it ran through the road in no time as Vishal's second son, Akshay drove it forward.

The SUV reached the airport. Akshay stopped the vehicle near the airport terminal and Vishal, Ashok Kumar and others took the luggage out of the dickey, and then, Akshay parked the SUV in the parking area. Then, all of them moved to the terminal, and later, Ashok Kumar and Arjun checked in at the airport building. Afterwards, they walked to ascend the plane after Vishal and his family bade them farewell, they had asked them to call them on again and they said, they would be very happy to receive them and Vishal and his sons cuddled Ashok Kumar and Arjun. Ashok Kumar had promised them that he would come to them again.

The plane landed at Mumbai airport on eight thirty in the night and all the air passengers began to descend from the plane along with whom, Arjun and Ashok Kumar descended from the aeroplane, they felt a feeling of nostalgia when they walked on the Indian soil again. They reached the terminal after all the procedures and they looked for Ashok Kumar's nephew, who had been asked to come with their car. They found him among the people who had come to greet and send off the passengers and they smiled to him and put their bags in the dickey of their car. The nephew asked Arjun and Ashok Kumar how they are and they too asked him how he is, and later, they ascended the car and it moved forward and then outside the airport compound.

Arjun, Ashok Kumar and Ashok Kumar's nephew, Atul reached their house shortly afterwards. They got out of the car and entered the house after Ashok kumar unlocking the door and they got in to the guest room and sat on the chairs there. Later, Arjun went to the kitchen and brought three cans of cold Red Bull and some cookies to the guestroom and placed them on the teapoy.

That night, Atul stayed with Arjun and Ashok Kumar in their house. They watched television and dined out from a nearby restaurant and went to bed when it turned to be 10 o' clock. When the morning spread, the three of them rose from the bed and ate breakfast later, they had brought the food from outside, the last day. It was corn flakes what they ate for the breakfast, which was prepared by Arjun by mixing milk powder with water and then the corn flakes, and coffee also was made by him. Ashok Kumar read the day's newspaper, when Arjun read one sheet of it and Atul another.

Arjun looked at the garden in front of the house and its surroundings with ardour that he is seeing it after days as there were so many flowers blossomed on the plants newly which brought a feeling of aestheticism to his mind.

Atul went from Ashok Kumar and Arjun a little later saying them goodbye and the father and the son became alone. They sat in the portico looking at the road in front of their house as they had got nothing to do, Arjun talked to his father and Ashok Kumar to him sometimes.

They ate lunch from outside going to a restaurant somewhat far, in their car as fine seafood was available there; they ate rice with crab fry and mussels with gravy inside the restaurant, which was the most sought after restaurant in the region. Later, they did not return home, but, went for a movie in a nearby cinema theatre, it was a Hollywood movie, Titanic. There were no much people in the compound of the theatre as the movie was not a newly released one and Ashok Kumar and Arjun got tickets easily, they entered the theatre and seated themselves in the backseat of the balcony. The film started in time and people watched it without making much noise.

Hollywood actor Leonardo Decaprio is shown on the silver screen and the spectators greeted him warmly; many of the spectators had watched the movie earlier and they knew the story. Arjun and Ashok Kumar too had seen the movie earlier, on the fifth day after it had been released.

After entering the ship, Titanic, the hero of the film, Jack is seen with his acquaintances and as the movie ran further, Jack sees a lady called Rose and they fall in love. People like to watch love stories rather than other stories. Many of the adults have come with their wives and there are a lot of youngsters and adolescents who have come with their girl friends, many of the adolescents and youngsters are dressed in tee-shirts, colourful shirts, jeans and other type of trousers and they wore different type of shoes as the girls too are not different and they are coming continuously though the picture had started earlier.

Ashok Kumar thought about his better half, he was missing her very much and Arjun contemplated on Pooja whom he loved intensively and decided to marry when he becomes older, Arjun also remembered his mother, seeing boys of his age coming with their mothers and fathers. Ashok Kumar thought about the days with his beloved wife and Arjun thought about his days with Pooja when they saw the love scenes between Jack and Rose, the first moment he saw kaveri came to Ashok Kumar's mind and the first night with her and the years after that, while Arjun reminisced the moment, he first saw Pooja. Pooja was the girl Arjun loved more than any other girls he had seen. He refreshed memory about the moments, they met each other during intervals at the school and the dreams both of them saw together and how he could not concentrate in his studies because of her.

Ashok kumar and Arjun turned to their left side hearing some loud voices which were of girls, they arguing with some boys. Everybody turned to where the sound was heard, they could make out, it was because some boys disturbed those girls and the girls reacting to it. They were some college students, sitting in front of some other college male students and one of the boys caught a girl in the darkness and the girl did not like it. The boys are claiming that they have done nothing and the girls are arguing that they are being harassed and others warned the boys not to do it again.

Intermission came and most of the spectators went out to refresh themselves; many of them bought tea, cool drinks and snacks. Arjun and Ashok Kumar too went out and bought refreshments, Ashok Kumar and Arjun saw some of their friends and they chatted with them. There were so many playful teenagers perambulating over the area, where two or three people sold food stuff, they were seen to be flirting and having a merry time when Ashok Kumar, Arjun and many others looked at them curiously, Ashok Kumar thought that Arjun too must be behaving like this when he is with his friends. Later, everybody returned to see the rest of the film.

After the interval, spectators sat on their seats when the teenagers made some noise as they did during the intermission and when the film resumed, the noise decreased as everybody did not talk much in order to drink in the movie. Later, Jack and Rose became united and the ship got wrecked as the film continued and later, the film ended, all the spectators got up from their seats and came out of the theatre unhurriedly as Ashok Kumar and Arjun too came out and they walked to the theatre compound. They could find people gathered in the surroundings, who have come for the next show. Ashok Kumar and Arjun reached near their car and they got in.

The car ran further and Arjun talked to Ashok Kumar about the movie. They did not wish to go home but wished to stay out until dusk. There was a ground near their house, where people played football in the evening; Arjun suggested to go there and see players playing. Ashok Kumar and Arjun used to go there before, in the evenings, there would be lots of spectators seeing matches who support each team. Arjun and Ashok Kumar knew that match would have started already and they decided to watch the rest of the play, they can meet many of their friends and natives there. As every others, Ashok Kumar and Arjun liked to be with a lot of people as they cloud be thus when they went to theatre, football ground and the likes.

The car reached the ground. Arjun and Ashok Kumar saw a big crowd around the ground where players played football obstinately, the crowd invigorated the players of each team. Though the players are amateurs now, they are really professionals who play for money normally. Arjun and Ashok Kumar joined the crowd and they too encouraged a team of which they were fans, the   competitors played obstinately giving passes to players of their team. Arjun an Ashok Kumar met many of their friends and acquaintances there among the people and they talked to them while watching the match.

There were boys and men selling eatables among the crowd, who approached everyone seeking whether they wanted something to eat, many of the viewers bought eatables from them and ate it as they watched the match at the same time. Arjun and Ashok Kumar did not buy anything for the time being. Later, the match ended as one team scored twice and emerged with flying colours when the other team failed to return the goals and the people on the winning side celebrated their team's success, Ashok Kumar and Arjun joined them as it was their team which won the match. The celebration lasted for long and it had become 7 o' clock when Ashok Kumar and Arjun came out of the ground.

Arjun and Ashok Kumar returned home afterwards when darkness permeated and they bought some food for them to eat in the night, from a restaurant on the way, which they used to go to earlier. Ashok Kumar bought Tandoori chicken, Tandoori rotti and Pepsi, and later, they reached their house and entered it after parking the car inside the shed, both of them sat in the guestroom and rested for some time.

At eight forty five, Ashok Kumar and Arjun ate the Tandoori chicken and rotti along with Pepsi, watching TV.

*　　*　　*　　*　　*

A couple landed in the Mumbai airport at 9 pm. It was Paresh and Divya who have come to india following Ashok Kumar and Arjun. Paresh was aware that Arjun and Ashok Kumar have come to India which he knew by asking Ashok Kumar when he met them in Qatar and he knew where they resided in Mumbai.

CHAPTER 10

It was a Wednesday. Arjun walked alongside the road. He, after one hour's playing cricket with his friends at the school after the classes were over, has come to the city not accompanied by anyone, and without going with his father to their house in their car. He had the objective to go home after spending half an hour in the city as he had to buy a novel, which is newly released and which is absorbing. Arjun moved to a book shop which was big and which contained a lot of books from various publishers, thinking about a particular book which was rated by readers very high at Amazon books, which he thought of buying from any book shop rather than buying online. He reached near the book shop, when a car stopped beside him and a man smiled to him lovingly. Arjun recognized the man instantaneously and he too smiled to him back. It was Paresh, who was alone in his car.

"Where are you going, Arjun?" Paresh asked Arjun amicably.

"Oh, I am going to this book shop," Arjun answered, turning his head in the direction of the shop, smilingly.

"Can I come with you?" Paresh asked him with an affectionate mien, raising his eyebrows.

"Oh, certainly," Arjun responded.

Paresh descended from the car after locking it and came near to Arjun after closing the door of the car; he looked at Arjun in the manner, a father looking at his son, with abounding love.

"Are you coming from school?" Paresh asked Arjun, seeing him carrying school bag.

"Yeah,"

"I too wish to buy some books, Arjun,"

"Okay then, we can go,"

"Yeah,"

But on walking a little further, Paresh turned to Arjun and said : "Can we put off going to the book shop to another occasion, Arjun? I want to talk to you. If you can come with me now, I would be much pleased,"

"To where?"

"We can go for a drive in my car, if you wish,"

Arjun did not speak, but, looked at Paresh's face smilingly.

"Don't worry, I will drop you at your house later," Paresh said in a consoling manner, looking at Arjun.

"Okay then, if you will not take much time," Arjun said as if he hadn't much time to spend with Paresh.

"No dear, only fifteen to twenty minutes," Paresh's words soothed Arjun and he became ready to go with Paresh.

Arjun ascended the car with Paresh and after some time, the car moved forward as Paresh drove it with medium speed. Arjun sat in the front seat with Paresh, he did not speak anything, but, he looked to the front, where there were a number of vehicles on the road and a lot of people on the roadside. As it was in the evening and was going to be dusk, the number of people and vehicles were in plenty and in all the shops, there were very much rush as many of the people did shopping. Paresh looked at Arjun several times, but, did not say anything; Arjun too did not speak though he too looked at Paresh one or two times.

The car rode further. It has become five minutes since the car got started and moved, both of them had to speak to the other, especially for Paresh who was overpowered with emotion as for what to say to Arjun.

"Arjun, I don't know where to start. Don't you remember what I said to your father when you were in Qatar?" Paresh started the talk between them.

"Yes," Arjun responded.

It has become four days since Ashok Kumar and Arjun reached home after their visit to Qatar and Paresh and his wife reached their home, the next day. Since then, Paresh had been looking for Arjun and this evening, he found out Arjun when he was going to the book shop.

"I really believe that you are my son. I will show you photographs of Deepak, then, you would believe me as you can see how much he resembles you," Paresh looked at Arjun much affectionately as he said.

Arjun felt much sympathy in his heart for the man. But, he knew the truth that his father had shown him his birth certificate, by which, he was convinced that his father is Ashok Kumar and not Paresh. Arjun feigned like believing what Paresh said that he did not like to crush the man emotionally with sorrow, that he knew that Paresh cannot stand it if he knew that he is not Deepak.

"Is it?" Arjun asked.

"You come with me to my house. I will show you the photos. Your mother is waiting there for you," Paresh invited Arjun to his house.

"But today, I cannot come. I will come another day,"

"My house is very near, you can just come and I will drop you later,"

"Okay then, let me call my father to tell him that I would be delayed," saying so, Arjun took his mobile phone from his shirt pocket.

Paresh felt sorrowful to hear Arjun saying 'my father' referring to Ashok Kumar, but, he did not show it outwardly.

Arjun called Ashok Kumar and said that he would be coming home late as he is going to the house of his friend. He did not mention anything about Paresh because he felt, that would be appropriate for the occasion; neither did Paresh tell him to say Ashok Kumar, the truth, that he feared Ashok Kumar may not like it.

"Do you know, how much I yearned to see you all these years?" Paresh looked at Arjun and said with a deep sigh.

Arjun looked at him as if acknowledging his sentimentality. He just smiled to Paresh.

"I wish to tell you about all my pains that I had after losing you," Paresh said with a sad facial expression.

Arjun listened to what he said, but, did not speak anything.

"Now that, I have got you back, do you know, how happy I am," Paresh continued.

After sometime, they reached in front of a house, which was somewhat big and painted in blue colour and there was a garden in front of it.

"Arjun, this is my house," paresh said to Arjun as he braked the car in front of the house.

"Yeah,"

They had not taken much time to reach there as Paresh's house was only about six kilometres far from the spot, where he met Arjun this evening. It was going to be twilight. Both Paresh and Arjun descended from the car and Paresh opened the gate of his house, he led Arjun to his house.

"Come Arjun, this is your house," Paresh said to Arujn smilingly.

Arjun just gave a smile and followed Paresh.

"Come inside," Paresh invited Arjun to his residence, which was closed and not anyone seen near it.

Paresh entered the portico and so did Arjun. Paresh rang the bell and waited; after sometime, a woman opened the door. It was Divya whom Arjun recognized easily as he had seen her at Qatar as she had come to Vishal's house with paresh when Arjun and Ashok Kumar were there.

Divya beamed to Arjun and Paresh as she saw both of them. She was as if surprised to see Arjun with Paresh.

"Arjun, do you know me?" Divya asked Arjun affectionately though she knew that Arjun knows her.

For a moment, Arjun remembered his mother, seeing Divya behaving to him as his mother behaved to him. His eyes got wet.

"Yes, I know. I remember." Arjun replied.

"Come inside," Divya said to Arjun.

Arjun was led to their guestroom. Both Paresh and Divya saw him with much fondness, they were in a state that they were not able to accept as true that their son has come back after years who was not to be found in spite of years' efforts. Arjun loved both of them though he knew, they are not his parents; he felt much sympathy for both of them, that they may not be completely confident that he is Deepak. But, he felt that Paresh firmly believes that he is Deepak, from his behaviour though Divya is not sure of it as he thought so from her conduct. Arjun was asked to sit on the sofa, and so, he sat being polite to Paresh and Divya.

Divya brought orange juice, some cakes and some biscuits after talking to him for some time. Paresh talked to him and later, he brought many snapshots of Deepak and gave them to Arjun, which Arjun looked at and got surprised to see the resemblance between Deepak and him and he looked at Paresh as he admitted, what he said is true.

"See Arjun, doesn't he look like you?" Paresh asked Arjun with raised eyebrows.

"Yes, he does," Arjun said.

"Now, you say, you are Deepak or not,"

Arjun said nothing, he just smiled.

"Arjun, you must comprehend that you are Deepak and not Arjun," Paresh said to the smiling Arjun.

"I understand,"

"So, now onwards, you should regard me as your father,"

Arjun looked at Paresh lovingly and Paresh was very happy that Arjun admitted to consider him, his father.

"Arjun, you eat the cakes and biscuits," Divya said to Arjun affectionately seeing Arjun not taking more cakes and biscuits.

"I have taken," Arjun said politely.

"Do you like to stay with us?" Paresh asked Arjun smilingly after some time.

"Yes, I would come to you," Arjun said.

"We would be much pleased if you tarry here with us," Paresh said, looking at Arjun with love.

"I will come occasionally. Now, you please drop me at my house, I am getting late," Arjun said, looking at his watch and then to Paresh, beaming.

"Okay, I will take you to your house, Arjun," Paresh stood up from his seat as he said, as he had been sitting near Arjun hitherto.

"Arjun, you should come to us daily," Divya said fondling Arjun.

"Yes," saying thus, Arjun too got up from his seat.

Divya was standing all these while near Paresh and Arjun. The three of them walked to the portico, Paresh and Divya embracing Arjun. After reaching the forepart of the house, Arjun said goodbye to Divya and Divya held him closely in her arms and later, he walked to the car along with Paresh. Paresh moved on foot at a fairly slow pace with Arjun, holding him close to him.

Paresh and Arjun got into the car. The car moved forward as Paresh knew the way to Arjun's house, Paresh looked at Arjun for a moment.

"Are you working in Qatar?" Arjun asked Paresh, turning to him.

"Yes, I am a teacher there," Paresh replied.

"Do you know, Ashok Kumar too is a teacher,"

"No, I did not know," Paresh felt blithe to hear Arjun calling Ashok Kumar as 'Ashok Kumar' rather than 'father'.

"He is working in the same institution, where I study," Arjun said as he thought his speaking would gladden Paresh.

"Is it?"

"Yes, he takes classes to me,"

"Which subject?"

"English,"

Darkness had pervaded far and wide. Paresh drove the car in a moderate speed. After a driving of twenty five minutes, they reached Arjun's house and Paresh stopped the car far from the abode in order Ashok Kumar not to see them.

"Don't tell Ashok Kumar about our meeting. He may not like it," Paresh uttered when Arjun was about to descend from the car.

"Yeah," Arjun said.

"Arjun, we should meet every day. I will come to you, my son," Paresh said to Arjun affectionately after Arjun went down from the vehicle.

"Yes, goodbye," saying thus, Arjun moved away from Paresh.

"Goodbye," Paresh too said.

Arjun walked to the house and reached it, when Ashok Kumar was seen waiting for him in the portico and Arjun entered the house later. There were lights in all the rooms and the portico.

"Why are you late, Arjun?" Ashok Kumar asked Arjun as he went in.

"Nothing dad," Arjun said.

Arjun sat in a sofa inside the guestroom. Ashok Kumar came to him and they talked to each other. As time passed, Ashok Kumar and Arjun ate supper and they turned in when it turned to be nine thirty.

CHAPTER 11

The next day, Arjun went to school with his father. As they reached the school, Arjun went to his classroom and Ashok Kumar to teachers' room. Arjun entered his classroom. The first hour was history, which was taken by a lady teacher called karishma; when she came to the classroom, every student stood up, respecting her. She was very beautiful that all the students, especially the boys looked at her glamour rather than listening to her class. She began to take class, which was about the British conquest of India, when all of the students looked at her face and when she wrote something on the blackboard, the boys looked at her, giving their opinions about her to others. Arjun's friends commented on her, Arjun too said something. All the girls looked at the boys with jealousy towards the teacher, that they wished the boys to treat them too like that.

Pooja looked at Arjun now and then that she was alarmed, Arjun would love the teacher more than her. Pooja was more beautiful than Karishma that Arjun loved Pooja more than any other females though he had infatuation for other ladies like Karishma. Arjun looked at Pooja too, that sometimes they met each other's eye mutually and they smiled to each other. Karishma is now facing the pupils, when they looked at her with a smile on their faces; she took the class as if avoiding the looks of the students. The boys looked at the girls too who are in their classroom at the same time as looking at the teacher. The boys and girls felt it to be very interesting to live like this, feeling love and behaving amorously toward the opposite sex.

Bell rang, informing everybody that the hour is over. The students are relieved after listening to the classes as listening to classes continuously brings discomfort to one's mind. There was no much time for them to relax as the next instructors came to their classes and began to take classes after the students standing up for one more time, the pupils are in a mood to go out as they are waiting for the interval to come, many of them did not listen to the classes though they pretended to be listening, teachers too are tired to take classes continuously. Arjun felt like others, to go out and refresh himself by talking, eating and drinking; he thought of talking to Pooja in the interval, which he liked very much.

Time elapsed. The second hour too is over and the teachers left the classes freeing the students; all the students, except some, who sat in the classroom conversing to each other, went out of the classroom to the outside of the school building. Arjun walked with his companions through the corridor to the cool bar to which they went daily, he saw many of his acquaintances on the way, who too were moving through the corridor.

There are many students everywhere in the school compound, conversing among themselves; the boys commented the girls generally and the girls acknowledged them shyly. There are bags of student mustered inside and near the cool bar, who are eating snacks and drinking something cool. Arjun ate a sandwich and drank grape juice with it as his friends also ate something or other and there were many of their classmates came there together.

There was only this one shop inside the compound, where the students could buy sweets, snacks and drinks and there was school canteen, where they and the teachers could get meals. So, every student in the school came to the cool bar in free time and there could be seen teachers also.

"Arjun, Pooja has not come yet. Why?" Richard, one of Arjun's close friends asked him, not seeing Pooja.

Normally, Arjun and Pooja met each other during intervals, before classes started and after classes ended. They were in deep love than what others thought about them to be, that they did not make their love visible much outwardly when they were with others, but, when they were in solitude, they showed to each other the real love they had in their minds, they were in such love that they could not but meet daily that in holidays too they tried to meet each other and called by mobile phone.

Arjun's close friends who were Richard, Sanjay and Vinay also had ladyloves whom they too met in free time. Their beloveds were not as beautiful as Pooja that they had slight envy towards Arjun; they called each other by the names of their girl friends.

As they talked to each other, Pooja came with her friends. She looked so pretty in her uniform too as she looked prettier in her colour dresses; she had done make up using face powder, lipstick and eyebrow pencil to her face to look more attractive. She and her friends gained access to the coolbar and stood inside it, as there were no seats vacant; Arjun and his friends vacated their seats and asked them to sit in as they had occupied four of the seats in the coolbar, earlier. Pooja and her friends sat in the seats though they denied first to sit, showing formality; Arjun, Sanjay, Richard and Vinay had stopped eating and drinking and they went to wash their hands.

Arjun talked to Pooja later, when he and his companions came back to her and her friends. Arjun asked her how she is and things like whether she liked the day's classes and did she watch the last day's cricket match; Pooja too asked Arjun something that she wanted to talk to him something or other. Arjun and Pooja felt proud to be noticed by others that they wanted to show others that they have got a friend who is good to look at and having a good character, Arjun felt gratified to hear others saying, Pooja is beautiful and Pooja too felt proud to be known as Arjun's girl friend. Others watched Arjun and Pooja as they talked to each other.

The bell rang and all the students began to return to their classrooms. Arjun and his friends strolled to their classroom, chatting to Pooja and her friends. Arjun's friends' girl friends were in other classrooms, and so, they could not see them always as Arjun perceived his girl friend, Pooja being in his classroom. The girl friends of Richard, Sanjay and Vinay had not come to the cool bar, and so, they could not see or talk to them, this day.

It became noon. After the forenoon classes, many of the students and many of the teachers went to the school canteen to where one could reach within three or four minutes from Arjun's classroom, Arjun, along with his friends went to the canteen, where there was chance them to meet Ashok Kumar as he too came there in the noon to have his lunch. At the canteen, Arjun met his father when he was eating lunch with his comrades and his father talked to him for some time. His father knew that Arjun is loving Pooja though Arjun had told his father nothing about that and Ashok Kumar asked him nothing about that; he knew it from others' talks and behaviour that they looked at Pooja and Arjun at the same time with a smile on their faces, when he was present.

Time elapsed, the day's classes are over. Arjun met his father in the evening and bought permission from him to come late to the house as he wanted to play cricket with his friends in the school ground, Ashok Kumar asked him, whether he should wait for him and Arjun said no, that he would be playing for more than one hour.

"Arjun, let me see you playing, I have no any business at home to go early," Ashok Kumar said to Arjun as sometimes, he used to watch Arjun playing, not going home early.

"Oh dad, then you come, I was going to ask you about that," Arjun invited his father, delighted.

Ashok Kumar liked to see Arjun bowling rather than him batting as Arjun was a terrific fast bowler that he generates so much pace that he may not be behind any of the fast bowlers who plays for the state of Maharashtra, but, his batting was average that he failed to gain a position in the district cricket team though he had participated in selection trials. Ashok Kumar had sent his son to coaching camp, but, as he was poor in his batting, Arjun did not continue going there, he was rather frustrated; Ashok Kumar too was sad that his son couldn't reach heights in the field of cricket, because of his poor batting, he had aspired much, Arjun to become a star cricketer. Ashok Kumar had yearned to become an Indian cricketer when he was a boy, that did not happen; then all his efforts was to make Arjun a famous cricketer, but, that too did not happen and he was terribly disappointed.

Ashok Kumar stood near the ground watching Arjun play. He had got a colleague of him to talk to, with him as he too was waiting for his son who is among those who played in terra firma and they watched the playing with fascination as seeing one's offspring, play is interesting. It was Arjun's team who bowled first and Arjun is the opening bowler who came running to the bowling crease and delivered a quick ball, which the opening batsman of the other team tried to defend but could not connect properly and the ball rested in the hands of the wicket keeper; everybody looked at Arjun with admiration when Ashok Kumar's colleague too looked at Ashok Kumar with acknowledgement. The batsman defended Arjun's next two deliveries successfully and scored a boundary in the fourth ball, but, he could not connect the next two deliveries amidst the accolades for his boundary.

Arjun's over has finished and he went to field near the boundary line, when the next bowler has been brought to the attack by the bowling team's captain; the new bowler bowled the next over and he conceded three consecutive boundaries after bowling three consecutive dot balls. Arjun fielded near where his father and colleague stood and he talked to his father something or other as Javed, Ashok Kumar's colleague talked to him about his bowling, he praised Arjun's bowling and said that it is so disappointing that he could not reach heights as he had talked to him so earlier too.

Arjun bowled his quota of two overs as it was a ten over match having seven players in each side. There were five bowlers in their team; all of the bowlers bowled their quotas. After one team's batting was over, they had scored seventy runs for five wickets and all the players rested for some time, sitting on the ground. Arjun's team was next to bat and their captain asked Arjun to open the innings. The players talked among themselves during the time, they rested. Ashok Kumar and Javed knew that Arjun was going to bat first and they encouraged him.

Arjun started batting as Ashok kumar, Javed and others watched him; there were a number of students and one or two teachers watching the game. Arjun defended the first ball he faced and scored a boundary in the second ball and he could not connect the next two balls and he scored a single in the next two balls, he received hand clapping for his boundary. The other batsman too scored a boundary in the next over and Arjun became out in the third ball of the fourth over within which he scored twenty runs. The match ended, Arjun's team scoring seventy two runs. The players on the side which won the match celebrated the victory with others and Arjun came to Ashok Kumar and Javed victoriously when Javed's son too came to them, who was in Arjun's team. Ashok Kumar and Javed congratulated their sons and later, they drank cool drinks from the coolbar, which was going to close. Later, all of them dispersed as Ashok Kumar and Arjun too went to their houses.

CHAPTER 12

        The next day, Arjun went to school not in their car but by bus that he had to buy something such as books, stationery, etc. He set out from home at eight forty five in the morning to the city as he had told Ashok Kumar about that; he reached the city at nine five and he went to a book shop, to where he went usually when he had the need to. After ambling along the road for some minutes, he reached the bookshop and he entered it, which was the same bookshop, where he met Paresh before and went with him to his house; he fossicked for books that he wanted among the books displayed there, where there were lots of book from various publishers. He wanted some academic books such as guides, work books and one pen and one colour pencil box, he also wanted to buy one or two novels. He got the academic books easily, but, he could not find the novel he wanted, and so, he looked for an interesting novel other than the one which he wanted, he found books such as The Actual by Saul Bellow, The Aguero Sisters by Christina Garcia, Already Dead by Denis Johnson, Bob the Gambler by Frederick Barthelme, Beach Boy by Ardashir Vakil, Cuckold by Kiran Nagarkar, The God of small Things by Arundhathi Roy, which won the Man Booker Prize for Fiction in 1997.

Arjun read the names of the books, its authors, the summary printed on the back of the novels and opinions of others written in the book in order to understand about the novels that whether they are worth reading; he wished to become an author himself that he liked others to read what he writes and he wished to get lots of money as he knew authors are making a lot of money these days. More than anything, he craved to gladden his father by becoming an author that he knew his father, yearning to make him someone in the society; he thought, though he couldn't reach heigts in the field of cricket, his father would be pleased to see him being a famous writer.

Arjun hadn't much time to spend there as he had to go to school which started at 10' clock, he selected two novels from the array of novels there and walked to the cashier, taking his academic books too with him. Totally, the sum was 1000 rupees to pay and Arjun paid the money giving the cashier a note of thousand rupees; Ashok Kumar gave so much money to Arjun for his needs as pocket money as he gave him five thousand or six thousand rupees in a month, though he did not get sufficient money as salary. As a child loves his parent more when he or she is given money, Arjun too loved his father more that he had indebtedness too toward his father.

As Arjun was exiting from the bookshop, he saw a man, coming to the shop, whom he recognized at once. It was Paresh. On seeing Arjun, Paresh smiled lovingly.

"I was looking for you, Arjun. Where were you?" Paresh asked Arjun.

"Oh, I had gone to school," Arjun replied showing intimacy.

"Did you buy books?"

"Yes,"

"I came here in the hope that you would be here,"

"Yeah,"

"You come with me, let us go somewhere,"

"But, I have to go to school,"

Paresh put his arm around Arjun's shoulder and walked with him to outside to the road.

"Today, you come with me, we can be with each other for a long time," Paresh looked at Arjun and said in a manner as he doubted whether Arjun liked his utterance or not.

"But, I have to go to school," Arjun told Paresh politely.

"Today, you don't go to school, you come with me,"

"I would have to inform Ashok Kumar,"

"Tell him on the the phone, that you have to go elsewhere," Paresh said.

"But, don't tell him that you are coming with me," after sometime Paresh said as he saw Arjun, not speaking.

"Okay," saying so, Arjun took his mobile phone from his pants pocket and dialled his father's number.

"Have you got any problem to take leave today?" Paresh asked Arjun as he was to talk to his father.

"No," replied Arjun.

"Yes Arjun," Ashok Kumar's sound was heard on the phone.

"Hello dad, I want to tell you something that I would not be coming to school today,"

"Why?"

"I met a friend of mine here in the city today and I am going to his house as he invited me,"

"Okay, I would be telling your class teacher about that,"

"Okay dad, I am disconnecting the phone," saying thus, Arjun disconnected the phone.

Paresh felt as if Arjun loving Ashok Kumar more from his talks and he was doubtful, whether Arjun has believed or not that he is his real father.

Paresh and Arjun walked to Paresh's car which was parked there on the roadside near the bookshop. Both of them ascended the car and Arjun sat in the front seat near Paresh. Paresh started the vehicle and it moved forward.

"First of all, we would put something away, Arjun, that I have not eaten breakfast today properly," Paresh said to Arjun as he drove the car.

"Why?"

"Because, I did not get time and I wished to buy you something and eat with you, if I find you,"

"That is nice,"

"We can go to that restaurant," Paresh pointed at a nearby restaurant and said.

"Okay, what would you buy for me?" Arjun asked Paresh with a smile on his face and eyebrows raised.

Paresh liked it very much, Arjun behaving to him intimately like this.

"What do you want?"

"Anything, you like,"

"Okay, now let us eat something light and in the noon we can eat Mutton Biriyani and in the evening, we can eat Fried Chicken,"

"Okay,"

"Now, we can go there and have some bread, butter and jam," saying thus, Paresh stopped the car close to the restaurant.

Arjun and Paresh entered the restaurant. They washed their hands and seated themselves face to face around a table. Paresh looked at Arjun and smiled that he wanted to give Arjun the love of long years; he remained looking at Arjun thus till a waiter came to them and asked them what would they have. Paresh looked at the man and asked whatever is there to eat, to which the waiter said names of several dishes and Paresh ordered bread, butter, cheese and jam looking at Arjun too at the same time, Arjun just smiled but said nothing.

"Arjun, do you know, how I had yearned to be with you like this or at least see you or at least know that you are alive," Paresh's eyes got slightly wet as he said thus after the waiter went.

Arjun looked at Paresh and smiled in a sympathetic manner.

"Arjun, I cannot really believe that you are sitting in front of me," Paresh continued, wiping his eyes lest others see him, being emotional.

"Now don't worry, try to forget the past," Arjun said pacifying words to Paresh.

"I cannot forget it, Arjun. You cannot imagine the pain one will have, if his or her child is lost," Paresh expressed the blues on his face when he said so.

Arjun said nothing, but, looked at Paresh's eyes compassionately. The waiter brought what they ordered and placed them on the table and Paresh and Arjun began to eat. Both of them did not speak anything while they ate. After having bread, butter, cheese and jam, Paresh and Arjun got up and laved their hands; Paresh paid the money though

Arjun asked whether he should pay and later, they came out of the restaurant.

"Where can we go now?" Paresh asked Arjun while they walked to the car.

"Anywhere you like," Arjun said smilingly.

"We will decide later, now we can go for a ride in the car,"

"Yeah,"

Arjun was loving the man more that Paresh showed him very strong affection of a father and his sympathy for the man increased as he knew how much he loved Deepak and how sad he became in the absence of him.

They ascended the car and Paresh steered it forward. There was no much traffic on the road and Paresh drove the car inside the city as he wanted to be alone with Arjun in the car, not going anywhere, where people thronged. Paresh and Arjun talked to each other as the car moved, Paresh was in a state of euphoria that he was so chuffed to be with Arjun that he is seeing him after years as he thought Arjun is his son. Arjun was happy to gladden this poor man who lived all these years yearning to see his lost son that he behaved like a son to Paresh and Paresh was so happy to see, Arjun behaving to him like a son comports to his father, though he had incertitude as to whether Arjun has credited that he is his real father, in spite of him behaving like a son and saying that he believes him to be his real father.

"I like to call you Deepak rather than calling you Arjun," Paresh said to Arjun, looking devotedly at his eyes.

"I like it, but, you call me thus when we are alone," Arjun said as if giving Paresh, a warning.

"Okay Arjun, I will call you so, only when we are alone,"

"Yeah,"

Time elapsed and it turned to be twelve fifteen when they reached near a delicatessen.

"Deepak, we can have something now," said Paresh, realizing that he is hungry and Arjun too would be hungry, seeing the restaurant.

"Yes," Arjun said.

Paresh and Arjun alighted from the car and Paresh locked the door; they walked to the restaurant unhurriedly. They ate Mutton Biriyani from there, and later, they went to the beach, where they walked on the sands for a long time, talking to each other. They sat on the sand, looking at the vast sea and unbounded sky.

"Arjun, I should have brought Divya too with me, she always talks about you," Paresh said to Arjun as if compunctiously.

"Why didn't you bring her?"

"I was not sure that I would meet you,"

"You bring her next time,"

"Yes, I would be bringing,"

For some time, they did not talk after speaking about Divya and later, Arjun spoke about going back when it turned to be three fifteen.

"Shall we go back?"

"Yeah, come. I will drop you at your house after eating something like fried chicken or pizza,"

They stood up and then walked to a pizza hut, which was nearby and put away one pizza each, which was tasty. Then, they uprose to the car and the car moved amidst people and other vehicles; there were a number of people all over the beach and its surroundings, whom Paresh did not heed as his mind was full of Arjun.

They reached Arjun's house after about two hours that they spent time in the city, going to malls and bookshops. Paresh did not buy anything for Arjun, fussing that Ashok Kumar would know about that, but, he gave Arjun

20,000 rupees as pocket money. Arjun said goodbye to Paresh and ambulated to his house, where Ashok Kumar was waiting for him. Arjun and Ashok Kumar talked and watched television for a long time, then, they spent time lying together in Ashok Kumar's bed and when it turned to be eight thirty, they dined supper and went to bed.

Arjun went with Paresh like this almost all days whenever they got a chance to, but Ashok Kumar, not knowing about all these.

CHAPTER 13

Days passed. Arjun went to school with his father and came back daily except in holidays. He met Paresh when he went to the city or somewhere else, that Paresh called him on the phone and apprised him, where he should come and they met each other in the destined spots. Paresh was so happy that Arjun loved him very much and considered him to be his real father; Arjun visited Divya too now and then and sometimes, Divya came with Paresh. This continued, but, Arjun said nothing about it to Ashok Kumar that he felt, it might be befitting for the situation and he decided to tell him later; Arjun loved Paresh much but it was Ashok Kumar, that he loved than his life, he being his real father, the love he had for Paresh was out of sympathy.

It was a holiday. Ashok Kumar and Arjun woke up early in the morning; Ashok Kumar bathed when Arjun read one of the novels, he bought from the bookshop, last time. He had read first few chapters of the novel and now he is reading the fifth chapter which was about the protagonist's love for his beloved. Later when it turned 7 o'clock, Arjun went to his bathroom in his room and bathed, when Ashok Kumar had not finished bathing; Ashok Kumar and Arjun slept the previous night in Ashok Kumar's room; before Ashok Kumar went to bath, Arjun had given him coffee and he too had had coffee.

After bathing, Arjun came to his father's room, wearing a brown colour shirt and blue jeans, when Ashok Kumar was reading the same novel that Arjun read earlier, he was reading the fourth chapter as he had read the first three chapters earlier.

"Where did you reach, dad?" Arjun asked Ashok Kumar about the novel.

"I am reading the fourth chapter now," replied Ashok Kumar.

"Isn't it interesting?"

"Of course,"

"Dad, where shall we go today?"

"Where do you want to go?"

"We can go to the city,"

"Okay,"

"We can visit any of our relatives,"

"Yeah,"

Ashok Kumar had worn new clothes, check shirt with brown, yellow and blue colours and pants of blue colour.

"Arjun, we can go after breakfast," Ashok Kumar said to Arjun smilingly.

"Okay dad,"

"What do you want for breakfast?" Arjun asked after sometime when his father said nothing.

"Anything you like, like bread and jam or cornflakes,"

"Then you come and sit in the dining room,"

"Okay,"

Arjun went to the kitchen and took a cornflakes package and put the contents to a bowl and poured some milk into it and added sugar; he brought it to the dining room and placed it on the table and he brought two empty bowls for him and his father. Then he returned to the kitchen and made tea for themselves, he brought two glasses of it to the table.

"Come on dad, I have made cornflakes for you," Arjun asked his father to come to the dining table.

"Okay," saying thus, Ashok Kumar came to the dining room, pulled a chair and sat on it.

Arjun too sat on another chair and ate breakfast with his father. After having breakfast and washing their hands, Ashok Kumar and Arjun came to the facade and sat in the portico for some time.

"Arjun, did you see that man, whom we met at Qatar, here?" Ashok Kumar asked Arjun as he thought about that now, Arjun had expected Ashok Kumar saying like that.

"No dad, he might not have come to India," Arjun told a lie, expressing sympathy for Paresh.

"I feel very sorry for him that I cannot stand it if I were in his position," Ashok Kumar said showing pity for Paresh.

"Do you like me, meeting that man?" Arjun asked Ashok Kumar thus, to know his mind.

"Yeah, he would be pleased to be with you," Ashok Kumar said, looking at Arjun's eyes.

"If I see him, I would be gratifying him," Arjun said, looking at his father.

"You should do that,"

Thenceforth, both of them did not speak for a while.

"Arjun, we can go out," Ashok Kumar stood up as he said after sometime.

"Yeah," Arjun said.

Both of them went inside the house and came back later. They were going to the city. Ashok Kumar locked the door from outside and Arjun and he ambulated to the adjacency of their car; both of them ascended the vehicle and within minutes, the car got started and Ashok Kumar drove it to the main road. They headed to the city amidst other vehicles when Arjun thought about Paresh that Paresh had called him by phone and asked him to come the city, to which Arjun said that he would not be able to come as he is going somewhere with his father.

Ashok Kumar and Arjun reached the city. They descended from the car and walked along the road after Ashok Kumar parking the car on the roadside. When they reached near a cool bar, two eyes saw them from far as those eyes were searching for these two, who went to the cool bar to have something cold. It was Paresh. It was not that he did not like Arjun going with Ashok Kumar but he wanted to know that whether Arjun considered him to be his father or he considered Ashok Kumar as his father. Seeing Arjun's conduct toward Ashok Kumar, Paresh thought as he is still regarding Ashok Kumar as his real father.

Paresh followed them to the cool bar. He covered his face with his hands and entered the cool bar where Arjun and Ashok Kumar was sitting; he sat two tables away from them, whom neither Ashok Kumar nor Arjun saw or recognized and he harked to what they were saying. Arjun and Ashok Kumar knocked back orange juice and talked to each other. Arjun behaved very lovingly to his father and Ashok Kumar back. Ashok Kumar put his arm on Arjun's shoulders and Arjun experienced the caring of his father like a bride within the hold of the bridegroom; Paresh was seeing all these with a feeling of jealousy that he thought Arjun must be feigning to him like he believed him to be his real father.

Paresh became too upset again that he had come out from his state of utter disappointment for years, losing his only son. He became so sad that he did not even think that Arjun must be pretending as loving Ashok Kumar to make him happy and he was almost to cry; he did not stay there anymore that he went out of the cool bar, still covering his face. He went to his car, crying inside his mind and ascended it in no time, he drove the car to his house. He did not want to tell anything to Divya that he feared Divya would say, why did he believe Arjun to be his son when there was no perfect evidence and he did not want to live any longer. He reached his residence and Divya received him; he showed no sign of sadness as he was accustomed to becoming sad all these years though not as much as this. Divya felt no doubt that Paresh had cried much when he was driving and he was able to not show his grief.

Paresh lay in his bed after drinking pineapple juice that Divya gave him, thinking about Arjun and Ashok Kumar that he believed firmly that Arjun is his son and Ashok Kumar must have got him from somewhere. He lay facing upward, looking at the ceiling for long with tears in his eyes and he thought, it might be because Arjun has no perfect corroboration that he is his father, he doesn't believe him to be his real father. He wished to anyhow convince Arjun that he is his real father, then only he would regard him as his real father; Paresh found no way to convince Arjun that he is his genuine father and he became very sad. He sobbed at times as he lay in the bed.

*   *   *   *   *

"Arjun, we can now call on your uncle," Ashok Kumar said to Arjun after them spending two hours in the city, doing shopping and just walking in the city.

"Yes dad," Arjun said.

Ashok Kumar intended to visit his younger brother Nikil who is living nearby.

"Then come, let us go," Ashok Kumar said.

They walked to their car which was parked on the roadside. They ascended the car as they reached near it and the car got started and it moved. The car ran to Ashok Kumar's brother's house in a moderate speed as Arjun looked around to see if Paresh was anywhere there; he did not see Paresh anywhere, he felt assuaged that if Paresh sees him with his father loving each other, he would be dismayed. Arjun looked at the shops and people, there were a number of foreigners everywhere in the city, seeing and talking to whom is very exciting; the foreigners were curious to see India, which was very different from their countries.

Ashok Kumar and Arjun heard Hindi songs as Ashok Kumar had turned on the stereo earlier. It was songs from the Hindi movie 'Aashiqui' which Arjun and Ashok Kumar liked the most among Hindi film songs. The car reached Nikil's house within a few minutes and Ashok Kumar stopped the car and he and Arjun descended from it and Ashok Kumar opened the gate of his brother's house.

Ashok Kumar had not intimated Nikil about his visit beforehand that he used to visit him occasionally. Seeing Ashok Kumar and Arjun coming, Nikil, who was watering the plants in front of his house, welcomed them warmly.

"Oh, what a surprise! Come, come,"

"We came to the city today morning, then we thought to come here," Ashok Kumar said to his younger brother smilingly.

"I was just watering the plants," Nikil said politely.

The three of them walked to the house. Ashok Kumar and Arjun sat in the chairs that were seen in the portico of the house as they were led by Nikil to be seated and Arjun took a box of chocolates out of a plastic bag, he carried.

"Where is Adithya and Sonu?" Arjun gave the box of chocolates to Nikil and asked referring to the two sons of Nikil.

"They are inside, I will call them," Nikil said smilingly.

Nikil went inside the house and after sometime Nikil's wife and two kids came to the portico.

"Hai uncle and Arjun brother, how are you?" Both the children Adithya and Sonu greeted Ashok Kumar and Arjun simultaneously.

"Fine and how are you?" Ashok Kumar and Arjun too greeted them.

Adithya was nine years old and Sonu seven years. Nikil's wife, Sonali smiled to Ashok Kumar and Arjun and they back to her.

Ashok Kumar and Arjun spent time there as Nikil and his family entertained them; they chatted and ate lunch, spending about one hour there. Later, Ashok Kumar and Arjun said goodbye to Nikil, Sonali, Adithya and Sonu and they set out to their house.

*   *   *   *   *

Paresh ate lunch with Divya and talked to her as usual, he did not give Divya any doubt that he had some plans in his mind that he had made up his mind to kill Ashok Kumar in order to win the love of Arjun. He thought about that several times that he knew Arjun would be so sad if he knows his father is dead, but, there was no any other way in front of him Arjun to love him like he loving his real father. He knew that, Arjun would not like another man as he loves his real father, but, as Paresh thought, he may not be sure who his genuine father is. Paresh thought that Arjun might be suspecting that Ashok Kumar is his real father as he may be doubting him too to be his real father; he thought, though Arjun would cry initially if he does not see Ashok Kumar, he would gradually be relieved and would start to love him as his real father. Paresh had determined everything and now there is no a going back.

CHAPTER 14

Arjun woke up at 7 o' clock in the morning, the next day. He bathed and changed his dresses and came to Ashok Kumar, who was reading the day's newspaper in the portico.

"Father, aren't you coming to school, today?" Arjun asked his father, who is in his school uniform.

"Yes dear," was Ashok Kumar's reply.

"You come and eat something,"

"Yes, I am coming,"

Arjun went to the kitchen and made omelette for him and for his father; he brought bread and omelette to the dining table, when Ashok Kumar came and sat there after washing his hands. Arjun too sat beside him and both of them began to eat.

They finished eating the breakfast and later, they went to school as Ashok Kumar too had bathed and changed his dresses earlier. Ashok Kumar drove their car to the school.

"Dad, will you teach me driving as I had asked you before?" Arjun asked Ashok Kumar enthusiastically as he sat with his father in the front; he liked to drive a vehicle that he had already asked his father to teach him driving.

"Okay, we can go to a ground and I will teach you," Ashok Kumar said as he liked Arjun's wish.

"Okay, can you do it today?" Arjun asked Ashok Kumar smilingly.

"Yeah," said Ashok Kumar.

The car ran further and reached the school afterwards and Arjun and Ashok Kumar descended from the car after it had been parked.

*   *   *   *   *

Paresh had got a gun, a revolver. He had bought it years ago and he had the licence to keep it. He was planning in his mind to kill Ashok Kumar by shooting him; he made up his mind to kill him without anybody noticing it. He thought of doing it when Ashok Kumar comes back from the school that he had already made it out that Ashok comes to his house in the evening in his car and sometimes Arjun too would be with him. Paresh purported to follow him in his car and shoot him from a distance when he stops his car in front of his house and descends from it. He decided to shoot him if Arjun is not with him lest Arjun understand that it is he, who killed Ashok Kumar.

When it turned 3 o' clock, Paresh set out from his house to the city in his car, carrying his revolver in his pants pocket. He said to Divya that he was just going out and behaved to her as normally. He drove his car somewhat speedily, he had thought that Arjun would be so sad when he knows that his father is dead and he had hesitation to do the murder as he was a nice human being. But, it was the love he had for Arjun, which brought around him to do this crime. Paresh did not think that he would have to go to jail if he is caught as the murderer as he usually did not think such things always, as his nature was thus.

Paresh saw Ashok Kumar when he was returning from the school and he followed him; he understood that Arjun is not with him and this is a good chance to kill him. Arjun was not in the car with Ashok Kumar that he remained at school to play cricket with his friends and he would be coming home afterwards. Ashok Kumar had bought cakes, chocolates and fruits to give to Arjun when he comes home; he thought always about his motherless child, who would be always bearing the pricks of bereavement of his mother.

After running for some time, Ashok Kumar's car reached his house and he descended from the car to open the gate of his house. Abruptly, four bullets dashed to him and pierced his chest as he turned to his backside. Ashok Kumar fell on the ground immersed in blood. Paresh after shooting, took his car forward and drove it very speedily. Ashok Kumar cried out of pain and he had died by the time people came running to him from the surroundings.

When Arjun came to his house, he saw people gathered in the yard of his dwelling from far. He had come by bus and he came walking to his house. From the deportment of the people, he conjectured that something terrible has occurred. He thought about his father that something must have happened to him; he quickly ran to his house to see his father.

"What is the matter? What happened?" Arjun asked the people with a worried face.

Those conglomerated there, did not say anything. They looked at Arjun sympathetically, their eyes were wet, feeling compassion for the boy and they felt sad to lose Ashok Kumar; they knew that Arjun has been deprived of his father too after his mother. Arjun understood that his father might have died from the behaviour of the people and he moved quickly into the house, where Ashok Kumar's body had been placed in the guestroom. Arjun could not believe his eyes. He cried loudly, tears erupting from the boys eyes. Arjun embraced his father's body violently that he was devastated emotionally. He cried loudly again and again calling his father. People didn't know what to do; they tried to console Arjun.

Ashok Kumar's body was covered with a length of cloth. Arjun did not know how he died; he was not in a state to ask about that to others. Ashok Kumar had died on the spot and those who came running, took him to his house and opened the door using the key, they got from Ashok Kumar's pants pocket; they did not take him to a hospital as he had died already and they informed the police after they covered his body with a cloth and made him lie in the bed. They knew it was a bullet injury and they made out, it is a murder. Ashok Kumar's neighbours and natives knew that there is no any possibility him to have any enemies that he was so gentle and nice to everyone; there was no any attempt for a theft either that they marvelled, who might have done this.

Later, police came and they examined the body after the people said to them what had happened. Police questioned everybody who saw Ashok Kumar after he fell on the ground, being shot; they questioned Arjun also who said he did not know whether his father had any enemy like those gathered there, who said the same thing. Police asked Arjun the telephone numbers of his relatives and they informed them about their relative's death and they came in immediately to Ashok Kumar's house. Relatives consoled Arjun, who felt much commiseration for the boy that it is a great shock to the adolescent who hadn't been relieved from the grief caused by his mother's death.

Nobody had seen who shot Ashok Kumar as there was nobody on the spot when the incident occurred and the police got no any clue as to who might be the killer; afterwards, police took the body to post-mortem and people dispersed when it turned to be night. Many of Arjun's relatives remained in the house, consoling him as much as they could, several others returned to their abodes as there was no enough space in the house for them to sleep there.

Arjun dined supper with his relatives, some of whom made chapathis and chicken curry. All of them were so sympathetic towards Arjun that he has lost both his father and mother and they felt so sorry for Arjun that they knew one cannot stand the grief of losing one's parents and living without them. Arjun went to bed at 9 o' clock to his father's room, heartbroken; he lay in the bed touching his face on the pillow. He did not wish to live in a world where his father is not, tears flowed to the pillow and it got wet. Arjun's uncle Nithin came to the room to sleep with him and he lay beside Arjun, consoling him; his consoling words somewhat lessened Arjun's pain. Time elapsed and he fell into sleep.

*　　*　　*　　*　　*

Paresh felt so guilty and he felt so sorry for Ashok Kumar and Arjun. He thought that he should not have done so, thinking about the condition of Arjun that the poor boy must be bawling now; he felt uneasy and had guilty conscience that he walked to and fro in his room. He showed nothing to Divya and behaved pleasantly to her and spent most of the time in his room thinking about Arjun that he has done unpardonable harm to him. His heart beat fast to go to Arjun and console him.

Paresh pretended that he did not know about the death of Ashok Kumar and he did not go there as he feared, people might suspect him to be the murderer; he wanted to see Arjun really badly that he wanted to console him, his hatred toward Ashok Kumar has decreased out of remorse. Paresh slept that night when there was half moon visible in the sky and a number of stars.

In the morning, Paresh woke up early and he did not know what to do. He was full of guilty conscience that he killed the father of a motherless child; he was thinking now only, the seriousness of what he did. He really became uneasy that he thought, he should not have done so. Paresh could not go for bathing, he couldn't eat breakfast properly and he was utterly remorseful.

Time elapsed, a thought occurred to Paresh that Arjun may go with any of his relatives to their house to live with them as he is alone in that house and he cannot live solitarily; he thought that something should be done in order to forestall that, otherwise he can't live with Arjun together. He determined to go to him and bring him to his domicile before he goes with somebody else. He went to Arjun's house when it turned 11 o' clock, after telling Divya that he is going to the city.

But on reaching Arjun's home Paresh saw people in the house and made out that the body of Ashok Kumar has not got into the residence after the autopsy from the talks of the people, who sat and cackled sitting in the benches adjacent to a nearby shop when he came there, descending from his car; so, Paresh headed to the city, proposing to come back afterwards that he was aware, it will take time Ashok Kumar's body to reach his house after the post-mortem, he now, stewed that there would be a police investigation as he thought about it now. He spent hours in the city and came back to Ashok Kumar's residence in the evening, but still, the body had not come, and so, he returned to his residence. He came to know, the body would be coming after days. After reaching his home, he spent time in his room, not talking much to Divya.

After two days, after waking up from sleep, Paresh bathed and changed his dresses and ate breakfast. He made up his mind to go to Arjun in the evening as he thought, by then, the last rites of Ashok Kumar would have finished and he can see Arjun when he would be lone and he intended to bring Arjun to his house to live with him and for that, he planned to tell Arjun's relatives that he is ready to adopt him.

Paresh doubted whether Arjun would have any dubiety as to he is the murderer that he would think, there is likelihood him to be the murderer as he may try to kill Ashok Kumar in order Arjun to love him more. Paresh spent time, watching television and reading a novel until the time he intended to go to Arjun.

CHAPTER 15

In the evening, Paresh went to Arjun's house. After travelling for minutes, he reached his house and he ambulated to meet Arjun who was with his relatives; Paresh rang the doorbell and Arjun came to him as the door was already open.

"Oh, sir you," Arjun said, seeing Paresh.

"Arjun, I knew about the death of your father late. I am sorry that I could not come earlier," Paresh spoke as if apologising as he saw Arjun.

Arjun's kindred came to the portico to see who has come. They smiled to Paresh and Paresh to them back.

"This is dad's friend," Arjun introduced Paresh to others.

"Oh I see, come inside," Nikil invited Paresh smilingly. All others smiled to Paresh.

"Thank you," saying thus, Paresh entered the house and sat in the guestroom.

"Where do you reside?" Arjun's another uncle, Rajesh, who is the brother of his mother asked Paresh as he sat beside him.

"Twelve or more kilometres from here," Paresh replied smilingly.

Arjun's relatives talked to Paresh, Paresh did not tell them the truth, he just said Ashok Kumar was his friend at Qatar. Paresh asked about the others too and made out, they were Arjun's uncles, aunts and their children; he was also told about the funeral that it was over and that Arjun had ignited the pyre of Ashok Kumar. Arjun too did not want his relatives to know more about Paresh other than that he is Ashok Kumar's friend because he thought it might appropriate for the situation.

After talking for more than fifteen minutes, Paresh presented his plan to adopt Arjun in front of Arjun's relatives, who consented it with gratification; Paresh told them that he would be pleased if they allow him to take Arjun with him this evening. Arjun's relatives were happy that they thought, this man who has no children, would look after Arjun very nicely and they felt Paresh to be resembling Arjun that one might think that he is his father. Arjun's uncle Rajesh asked Arjun to go with Paresh, taking his possessions with him; he said to Paresh that they would be selling this house of Ashok Kumar and they would give the money to him, which he can use to take care of Arjun.

Paresh awaited for Arjun until he came to him with all the things, he needed. Arjun took with him his dresses, books and the likes and took them to Paresh's car as he was asked to do so by Paresh and he came back to his kindred to bid them a fond farewell, who gave him a send off to live with Paresh; they had thought earlier to take him with them that he would be living with any of his relatives, they were glad that Arjun would be happy to get a new father and mother who would look after him like their own son. Arjun once again came to his father's room, where his father and mother slept when they were alive and he could not but sob by the thought of leaving this room and this house where he lived with his parents for long years; he took his parents' photo from the wall, in which he was standing in the middle in between his parents and he kissed them with tears in his eyes. He took with him other photos of his parents and albums, containing his parents' and his photos.

Arjun went with Paresh to his car as his relatives looked at them, coming near to the gate; Arjun waved his hands at them, they had said to him that they would be coming to visit him whenever they get free time and had asked him to come to them when he is free. Arjun closed the gate and ascended the car with Paresh and the car moved; Paresh looked at Arjun in a solacing manner and Arjun simpered to him.

"Don't worry Arjun, think that you have got a new father and mother," Paresh said to Arujun while he drove the car, in a soothing manner.

Arjun just smiled but said nothing.

Paresh again said something or other to Arjun to console him that he saw his eyes awash. Paresh said that they were going to the city in order to buy something for Arjun and he drove the vehicle to the city. Arjun was lost in thought about his father, he didn't wish to live without him, but he did not show it outwardly and conducted like he wished to live with Paresh.

Paresh and Arjun reached the city shortly. They went to a biggish shop of apparels as Paresh wished to buy dresses for Arjun; they entered the shop which was one among a number of shops located there in a row. It was an attire shop, exclusively for Wrangler, where one could get shirts, T-shirts and jeans, there were bags of clothing in different designs and colours which adolescents like Arjun would like to have. A salesman asked Paresh whatever dresses they would like to have and Paresh told him, he wants shirts and jeans for adolescents, showing Arjun to him and the salesman showed dress items to them, which were for boys above the age of twelve.

After buying dresses, Paresh and Arjun came out of the shop. Paresh bought two shirts, one T-shirt and two jeans for Arjun and he bought one shirt and one pants for himself when Arjun asked him to buy; later, they went to a shop selling shoes and sandals and bought shoes and sandals for both of them. Then, after buying chocolates and fruits they headed to Paresh's house in the car.

The car reached Paresh's house and both Paresh and Arjun descended from the car; Arjun opened the gate and Paresh drove the car into the compound and he parked it in the shed, which had been located at the left side of the dwelling. Paresh rang the doorbell while Arjun looked around to see the surroundings in the realisation that he is going to live the rest of his life there and after some time Divya opened the door and received Paresh and Arjun, who were standing near the door as Arjun too had come there after Paresh.

"Arjun, why have you taken all these bags with you?" Divya asked Arjun, seeing three or four bags with him and Paresh, which Arjun and Paresh had taken from the car.

"He is going to live here today onwards," Paresh said to Divya smilingly.

"Is it? Has his father assented for that?"

Paresh did not speak for a while. Arjun looked at Divya, simpering.

"What happened? Why don't you speak?" Divya asked to Paresh and Arjun that she suspected something must have happened to Ashok Kumar.

"Ashok Kumar is no more," Paresh said as if sadly.

"What happened to him?" Divya turned curious.

"He died in an accident," Paresh lied as he had told Arjun to tell Divya that it was an accident.

Divya looked at Arjun in a manner that she could not believe how he would bear this.

"How did it happen?" Divya was so sympathetic about Arjun when she asked so.

"The car in which he travelled hit a lorry and he died," Paresh told Divya showing sympathy for Ashok Kumar.

"When did it happen?"

"Two days ago, but, I knew it only today,"

"I went to his house and there were Arjun's relatives to whom I said that I was ready to adopt him," Paresh continued as Divya did not speak.

Divya pacified Arjun, patting gently over his head; she felt so sorry for him that how can a boy of his age stand this grief of losing his father and mother. Arjun entered the house with Paresh and Divya and he placed his bags on the floor.

"Arjun, bring them, I will show you your room," Paresh led Arjun to a room, taking one of his bags with him.

Arjun took his bags to that room, which was of a moderate size and he placed them there. Divya followed Arjun and Paresh. There were three bedrooms in that house, two of them unoccupied as one was for guests and the other one was maintained for Deepak to stay, if he is found at any time. Arjun had already seen this room when he came earlier to this house with Paresh.

There was a bedstead with a bed over it, a table, a chair and a cupboard in that room; there was ceiling fan and air condition in the room and it was bath attached.

"Did you like your room?" Paresh asked Arjun smilingly.

"Yes," said Arjun looking at the bedstead, table and other objects in the room. He knew that the couple keep up this room for Deepak if he comes ever.

"You please remain here for some time, Divya will bring you something to drink. I will come right now," Paresh went to his room, saying thus after sometime.

Arjun sat in the bed. There were two windows in that room. He looked outside through the window, darkness had permeated everywhere. In the night, he stood there alone for some time that Divya had gone to the kitchen earlier together with Paresh, who went to his room; there was slight breeze outside the house which he experienced as the casement was open, outside the house, there could be seen several trees and plants.

"Arjun, have this," It was Divya who came to the room with a glass of grape juice.

"Yes," said Arjun and he bought the glass from Divya.

"You lie in the bed for some time after drinking the juice," Divya said looking at Arjun affectionately.

"Yeah,"

"You would get relief if you lie for some time,"

Arjun gave the empty glass to Divya after belting down the juice. He lay in the bed after Divya went with the glass. Arjun tied both his arms at the back his head and lay facing the ceiling, he looked back on his parents. Mental pictures of his parents fondling him when he was young came to his mind; his eyes had begun to wet more.

"Arjun come, we can dine," Arjun woke from his thoughts hearing Paresh's words after some time.

"yeah," Arjun said courteously getting up from the bed.

Paresh moved to the dining room, to where Arjun came later.

"Look Arjun, we have got chapathis and mushroom curry, don't you like them?" Paresh asked Arjun smilingly as Arjun sat in the chair beside the dining table.

"Yes," said Arjun.

Paresh put three chappathis in Arjun's plate, which Arjun had taken and placed in front of him.

"You try this mushroom curry that Divya cooked, it is really tasty," Paresh said, pouring some mushroom curry to Arjun's plate.

Arjun ate the chappathis and mushroom curry which was dainty. After dining, Paresh and Arjun came to the portico and sat there, looking at the darkness in front of their house; there was light in the portico and in the front part of the house as the things near the house were visible. Paresh was thinking that how lucky he is to get Deepak back, he solaced himself that Arjun would be relieved over time from the grief of losing Ashok Kumar and Kaveri and would begin to live as his and Divya's son. He looked at Arjun, who was looking at the plants and flowers in front of the abode, Arjun too looked at Paresh at times. Paresh asked Arjun something or other and Arjun gave answers to them; Arjun did not talk much, he remained reticent most of the time. Divya came to them and seated herself beside them, who too had dined with them. Arjun thought about his parents when Paresh and Divya thought about Arjun that they were very happy to get their son back as Divya too had suspicion that Arjun is their own son when Paresh firmly believed Arjun to be his son. Both Divya and Paresh sympathised with Arjun that how sorrowful he would be.

CHAPTER 16

Two weeks went by. Arjun began to go to school from his new house, Paresh took him to school in the morning after Divya groomed him, dressing him in his school uniform, combing his hair and the likes as she felt Arjun to be Deepak in his young age before they lost him. Arjun had begun to live with Paresh and Divya as their son, or at least he pretended to live so, though in his mind, he loved his parents far more that he was not able to see anyone else in their place. He went to school and came back home daily, in free time, Paresh, Divya and Arjun went outside the house to beach, cinema theatre and the likes.

That morning Arjun woke up very early, it had become five thirty. He looked outside through the window, where there was   darkness and he felt cold as it was winter in that part of the world. It was a holiday and Arjun liked to lie in the bed for more time, but, he sat in his chair for some time that he wanted to bathe early. He thought, he may fall into sleep if he lie again. He turned on the light in his room and took a novel from the table, which he had read the first fifteen chapters and just read once again what is printed on its back; it was a sob story in which the protagonist is tormented by his step mother, Arjun put the book on the table after sometime and rose to his feet.

Arjun went to bathe and he came back shortly. He dressed in T-shirt and jeans which Paresh had bought for him the day they came here from Ashok Kumar's house; he dressed those dresses in order to tickle Paresh pink, though he liked to put on the dresses that his father had bought him. Arjun looked in mirror, combed his hair and took his wallet from inside the cupboard and opened the room's door and went to the portico. He opened the door and sat in the portico tying his arms at the back of his head; he experienced the cold which he liked very much as he was keen about waking up in early mornings that the feeling one gets during this time is exquisite.

Time passed. Paresh came to the portico when it turned seven thirty and he stood beside Arjun.

"Arjun, did you drink something, coffee or tea?"
Paresh asked Arjun affectionately.

"No dad," Arjun called Paresh, 'dad' as Paresh
made him call thus, telling him that he liked to be called like
that.

"You go to Divya and she would give you,"

"Yeah, did you drink something?" Arjun asked
Paresh as he stood up.

"Yes, I did," Paresh said.

Paresh went near to the gate to take the day's
newspaper which the paperboy had put there, after Arjun
went to Divya. Arjun had not noticed the newspaper lying
there.

A thought came to Arjun's mind that he, Paresh or
Divya had not visited all of their relatives hitherto, though
they had visited some of them; some of Arjun's relatives had
come to them too, though not all. Arjun wished to tell about
that to Paresh and he went to Paresh with the mug of coffee,
which Divya had given him; when he entered the portico,
Paresh was reading the newspaper.

"Dad, shall we visit my relatives today as today is a
holiday?" Arjun asked Paresh standing near him.

"Yeah, we shall visit the rest of the relatives whom we haven't visited yet," Paresh said, raising his head and looking at Arjun.

Arjun sat in a chair beside Paresh when Paresh asked him to; Arjun respected Paresh as he had set store by Ashok Kumar that he stood up when Paresh came to him, if he was sitting already. He only sat when he was asked to, when he came to Paresh, if Paresh had been sitting already.

Paresh was timid to face Arjun's relatives as he dreaded to face Divya and Arjun that they might suspect him to be the murderer of Ashok Kumar; he feared, Arjun and Divya might suspect him that he must have killed Ashok Kumar to own Arjun, especially Arjun, that he knows that Ashok Kumar is murdered.

Arujn had a suspicion in his mind about the murder of Ashok Kumar that there was chance Paresh to kill him, but, he did not suspect Paresh much, realising, Paresh hadn't the need to do so that he had behaved to him as he behaved to his real father; Arjun thought that there is no chance, Paresh to be jealous of Ashok Kumar that he had told him that he has believed him to be his real father by seeing Deepak's photographs. Still, he had slight suspicion that Paresh would have murdered his father because his nature was thus. For that very reason, Arjun had hatred towards Paresh and he did not like to stay in his house; as he was not sure that Paresh is the murderer, he had love and indebtedness toward him that he adopted him when he was deprived of his parents, loved him excessively and bought him whatever he wanted. As for Divya, she hadn't much suspicion on Paresh, thinking, it was an accident.

After breakfast, Paresh, Divya and Arjun came out of the house. They were going to Arjun's relatives' houses; Paresh and Divya ascended their car. Arjun opened the gate and Paresh took the car outside their compound to the main road and Arjun closed the gate and got into the car.

"To whom shall we go first, Arjun?" Paresh asked Arjun as he was to take the vehicle forward to the left.

"We shall go to Rajesh, who is the brother of my mother," Arjun told Paresh as he sat in the front seat.

"To left or to right?"

"To the left,"

"How far is it from here?"

"About eight kilometres,"

Paresh drove the car to the left side. The time was eight thirty then and it would not take much time to reach Rajesh's house, they would be reaching there within fifteen or twenty minutes. Paresh, Divya and Arjun had opened the glasses of the car and cold wind was blowing to the inside;

Arjun looked outside to see people, shops and scenery just as Divya and Paresh, who too was looking outside.

They reached Rajesh's house within minutes. Paresh, Arjun and Divya alighted from the car and Paresh parked it on the roadside and three of them walked to Rajesh's residence after Arjun opening the gate; Paresh rang the doorbell and a woman opened the door after sometime.

"Oh Arjun, it is you?" the woman, who was Rajesh's wife exclaimed seeing Arjun, Paresh and Divya.

Arjun, Paresh and Divya smiled, and later, entered the house when they were asked to.

"Please be seated," Rajesh's wife asked them to sit, leading them to the guestroom.

Rajesh's wife Amisha brought out to Arjun, Paresh and Divya for some time, and then, she brought tea and snacks for them. Arjun loved to come by his relatives that they were the brothers and sisters of his parents and he loved them very much; when he sees them, he is delighted like seeing his parents for they have blood relation with his parents.

Amisha told them that Rajesh was bathing and he would be coming soon. Rajesh came to them later and was surprised to see Arjun, Paresh and Divya, he sat with them and conversed. Paresh introduced Divya to Rajesh as he had already introduced her to Amisha; Divya went to the kitchen with Amisha and they talked to each other when Rajesh and Paresh chatted among themselves; Arjun did not talk much, he just listened to what Paresh and Rajesh was saying. Rajesh's and Amisha's children were not there as they had gone to the city, which Rajesh mentioned to Paresh, Divya and Arjun. Arjun stood up from his seat and went to the other rooms of the house and then to the yard in front of the house.

"You should go only after lunch," Arjun heard Rajesh saying thus to Paresh when he came back to the guestroom.

"We will come another day, today, we have to visit Arjun's other relatives," Paresh wished to go from there anyhow that he feared Rajesh and his wife may suspect him.

"Is it? Then you should certainly come another day to spend more time here," Rajesh said looking at Arjun too.

"Certainly," said Paresh smilingly.

"Arjun, how do you feel now?" Rajesh asked Arjun affectionately, he hadn't talked much to Arjun before.

"Feeling better," Arjun replied with a smile on his face.

Rajesh hugged Arjun to him and remained thus for sometime; Arjun was about to sob, but, he did not show his emotion outside.

Afterwards, Paresh, Divya and Arjun took leave of Rajesh and Amisha. Rajesh and Amisha went to the gate to bid Arjun, Divya and Paresh farewell and Paresh and others ascended their car after waving hands to Rajesh and Amisha, when Paresh remembered a thing that they had not bought anything such as fruits and chocolates to give to Rajesh's children and he said about it to Divya and Arjun afterwards as the car moved; Arjun and Divya too felt uneasy about it that what would have Rajesh and Amisha thought, they bringing nothing with them when they came for the first time, Rajesh and Amisha had come to Paresh's house earlier and they had brought fruits, chocolates and cakes to them. They had forgotten to buy something and this thought discomforted Arjun, Paresh and Divya greatly throughout the day.

Neither of them talked further as the car moved after Paresh asked Arjun where to go next. Arjun said that he would like to go to Nikil, who is Ashok Kumar's younger brother. They bought chocolates, pastries and fruits, stopping the car near a shop, this time not forgetting to buy something for the hosts. Within minutes, they reached Nikil's house and they descended from the car after Paresh parking it on the roadside and they ambulated to the abode after opening the gate. Nikil, his wife and children were sitting in the portico and when they saw Paresh and others coming, they stood up to take them in; Paresh, Arjun and Divya entered the house and was led to the guestroom, they sat in the chairs. Arjun gave the kids the plastic bags of what they bought for them. Neither Nikil nor his wife nor his children had seen Divya before and Paresh introduced her to them. They talked for minutes and later, they ate lunch together; then, Paresh said they are leaving now and would come another day. Paresh had come to both Rajesh and Nikil out of fear too that others would suspect him, if he did not; anyway, he was not able to not come, fearing that others would think ill of him.

Paresh, Arjun and Divya took leave of Nikil and his family. Then, they visited one more relative of Arjun, and then, they returned home; they reached home in the twilight when it had turned seven o' clock. They entered the house after Paresh opened the door with the key. They had dined out in the evening and none of them wanted food in the night. Arjun went to his room and lay in his bed, he had turned the air condition on and he covered his body with the blanket; the windows in his room had been closed and he did not look outside through them. Arjun thought about his parents, he marvelled why god took both of them away from him, though, he had not sinned even a bit. Tears rolled down from his eyes.

CHAPTER 17

Days passed by. Arjun went to school and came back daily. Paresh's leave was to expire and he has to go back to Qatar, he decided to take Arjun too with him and Divya and join him in any of the schools there; only a week was left for him to return and he took the measures to make Arjun quit from the school, now he is going. Arjun remained in his house after he retired from the school; Paresh and Divya was happy, Arjun to be with them the whole days.

Arjun went outside alone and with Paresh and Divya and remained in his house watching television and reading books; he had his laptop with him, which Ashok Kumar had bought him and he watched that too occasionally. He watched film songs, movies and many other videos in the internet as he had watched them when he lived with his parents. There were a number of videos in the internet showing different countries and one could get almost all the information one needed, from it.

It was a Sunday. Arjun woke up early in the morning and bathed. He came to the guestroom after he put on his clothes, which was shirt and pants and he drank coffee, which Divya gave him. Paresh was reading the day's newspaper in the portico and he came to Arjun later and handed him the newspaper over. Arjun read the newspaper and later, he ate breakfast with Paresh and Divya.

Arjun went to the yard of the dwelling and spent time looking at the plants and flowers; there were a lot of different kinds of plants in the front yard which bore different kinds of flowers. He watered the plants with a hose and cut the leaves of some plants with a pair of scissors, which he brought from the kitchen, in order them to look better and uniformly with every other plants. Later, he went to a nearby shop after mentioning Paresh about it and when he reached there, there were several boys, adult men and women there, who had come to buy things and he smiled to everyone, some of whom knew who he was and some did not who he was. Arjun waited there to buy a bath soap and a pen, during which he talked to his acquaintances, who behaved to Arjun very friendly and sympathetically that they were aware, he is an orphan.

After buying the things he wanted, Arjun returned to his house, where Paresh and Divya were standing in the garden. They smiled to him and he back to them.

Arjun went to his room and placed the bath soap in the bathroom as the soap he was using had expired, he put the pen on the table and sat in the bed. He didn't like much to go to Qatar with Paresh and Divya, he did not like to leave his native land, the place where he once lived with his father and mother; Arjun used to go to his old house where he lived with his parents occasionally when he went outside alone from Paresh's house. He would stay there for long whenever he went there; the house was locked and so, he would spent time in the yard. He would feel like his parents coming to him and fondling him when he stays there and he would feel like hearing his parents' affectionate talks to him. Arjun did not want to go to Qatar as he cannot go to his old house, if he went to Qatar, where there are remembrances of his parents.

Time passed. Arjun ate lunch with Paresh and Divya, and later, he rested in the guestroom. Paresh too was taking his ease with him and he was reading a book when Arjun went to the the kitchen to drink some cold water after sometime. On coming after drinking water he happened to see a book, which had a portrait of a man on its cover, in Paresh's and Divya's bed as the door of the room was open and he just entered the room to check the book; he used to go to Paresh's room earlier too when Paresh and Divya lay there as they liked him coming to them and they used to invite him to their room. The book was a novel with a stunning painting on its front cover, which Arjun liked very much, he turned its pages and he found it to be a lengthy novel which had four hundred and fifteen pages. Arjun read what was printed on its back cover and he made out the novel had got a good story.

Arjun read the first page of the first chapter of the book and put the dog-eared book aside, cerebrating to read it another time. The novel was an old one which Paresh had bought years ago. Arjun looked for other books which he may not have seen hitherto as this novel, Paresh had shown and said Arjun about all his possessions but forgot to show him few things, this novel was one among them. Arjun searched inside the cupboard, which was located in one of the right corners of the room, of which the door was not locked. He found the majority of the books to be familiar to him and he saw an octavo among the books of which the colour was red and he took it out of curiosity; he made out, it was a personal book of Paresh only after he read the first three words written in its second page which was as 'FORGIVE ME DEEPAK'

Arjun turned pages of the octavo that he turned curious to know why Paresh wrote like that. He put all the books in the cupboard just as they were earlier and closed the cupboard's door and he placed the novel which had a painting on its cover in the bed just as it lay there earlier and he stealthily went out of the room, not giving any suspicion that he had entered the room, he put the small book in his pants pocket, not showing it outwardly.

Arjun went to his room with the book. He had suspicion that Paresh might have killed his father and it might be because of repentance that he wrote like this in this book. Arjun entered his room and closed its doors and locked it in no time. He sat in the chair and put the octavo on the table;

he opened it and read again the first three words. There was ample light in the room as the windows were open.

Arjun turned a page after the second page of the book where there was written as 'FORGIVE ME DEEPAK' and he found some paragraphs written in the next page, he read it. The first paragraph read like this : "Deepak forgive me. I have done to you an unpardonable harm that I killed your father. It was only for winning your heart that I could not stand you loving Ashok Kumar than you loved me. At that moment, no other thoughts came to my mind other than to kill your farther, but now I repent to a great extend that I killed the father of a motherless child. I did not think that you would be this much sad. I am writing this with utmost remorse." Tears rolled down from Arjun's eyes swiftly through his cheeks and he sobbed intermittently.

Arjun stopped reading for a short while and put his arms on the table and then his head over it and remained thus for long. He cried for a long time remaining in that position, then he raised himself and resumed reading the next paragraph.

The next paragraphs read like this : "Deepak, I don't know, whether you know, I am of a different nature that all the thoughts would not come to my mind always and I act on the spur of the moment. I did this murder like that, that at that time I only thought of killing Ashok Kumar. I don't know whether you would forgive me or not.

It was later that I recognised, it would be a great shock to you and I saw you lamenting over it to a very large extent. I did the murder in order you to love me like your real father, forgetting Ashok Kumar. It was when I realised that you loved Ashok Kumar more in spite of all the love that I gave you and showing you Deepak's photographs.

Deepak, it was only after the murder that I made out that you grieve so much, losing Ashok Kumar. I had not expected that you would cry this much; I thought you will not have this much sorrow. I anticipated that you would love me more and regard me as your real father.

I don't know whether I should show you this book or not. I don't know how you will react. I feel so sorry for Ashok Kumar too,   I think, he would not spare me if he comes to life again.

Deepak, don't feel hatred towards me, I cannot stand it if you hate me. Please forgive me, Deepak. Please think, that it happened and I cannot give you Ashok Kumar back. Please forgive me, Deepak. Yours lovingly, Paresh."

Arjun read the writing completely, with a heavy heart. He did not wish to live any longer. He thought of killing himself. There was a small bottle of poison inside the cupboard, which he had purchased anyhow to commit suicide that he was always thinking of killing himself from the moment, he saw the dead body of Ashok Kumar.

Paresh had gone to his room earlier and he lay with Divya in the bed. They had no any suspicion that Arjun had come to their room and taken the book. Divya did not know anything about the book. Paresh had placed the octavo in the cupboard thinking, let Divya and Arjun see the book and read it, if they open the cupboard that he was so remorseful and wanted to tell Divya and Arjun, what he did.

Paresh went to the portico after sometime when the doorbell rang. It was his friend who came and Paresh smiled to him and he smiled back to Paresh; the middle aged guest was one of Paresh's best friends and Paresh led him to the guestroom. The man, Abhishek sat in the guestroom and talked to Paresh. Paresh is seeing him after long that he was in America, working there as an engineer, Paresh expressed his feeling of not seeing him for long. Divya came to them and talked to Abhishek as both of them were familiar to each other; she went to the kitchen and brought two glasses of orange juice and snacks. Abhishek expressed his regret to Divya, for having not brought his wife and children with him, he said, he could not bring her because she was not with him for the past one week that she had gone to her house.

It was to invite Paresh and Divya to his daughter's wedding that Abhishek came. The marriage ceremony is to be held after two weeks at his residence and Abhishek requested Paresh and Divya to come early to his residence, before 5 o' clock pm as the function is to be held at night; Paresh and

Abhishek expressed themselves to each other on several things and Abhishek said, he wanted to go soon as he has other engagements and he took leave of Paresh and Divya after sometime. Paresh and Divya went upto the gate to send Abhishek off and Abhishek left in his car, which was parked on the roadside. Abhishek had given his word to Paresh and Divya that he would be coming to them with his wife and children to stay with them for a longer time. It was only after Abhishek quitted that the couple remembered about Arjun; they felt uneasy, not to have said about Arjun or shown him to Abhishek. Paresh and Divya were as if in the days when they had neither Deepak nor Arjun with them.

CHAPTER 18

It was then, Paresh remembered a thing that he and Divya had been invited to a wedding of his friend, occurring this evening. The function would start at 5 o' clock and would be prolonged to 9 o' clock to 10 o' clock in the night.

"Divya, don't you remember that my friend, Irfan had invited us to his wedding today?" Paresh asked Divya to remind her of the marriage ceremony.

"Yes, I was going to tell you about that," Divya replied smilingly.

"It is already five, you get ready fast. There is a running of half an hour to reach there, he has asked to come early"

Both Paresh and Divya had spoken on Arjun about they   forgetting him when Abhishek came.

"You inform Arjun," Divya said to Paresh as she went to her room.

"Yeah," said Paresh and he went to Arjun's room.

Paresh knocked at the door. Arjun did not open the door. As Paresh knocked again and again, Arjun opened the door.

"Yes dad," Arjun did not show any traces of sorrow.

"Arjun, one of my friends had come. I forgot to introduce you to him,"

"Oh, that is all right. What is his name and when did you first meet him?"

"He is an old friend of mine. He came to invite us for the wedding of his daughter,"

"I see,"

"Now, I want to tell you one thing. Get ready, that we have to go to another marriage ceremony now,"

"Of whom?"

"That also one of my friend's. Don't you remember that he came here days ago,"

"Yeah, Irfan sir. But, I am not coming dad, I have got a headache," Arjun feigned to be having headache, touching his right hand on his forehead.

"When did you get a headache?" Paresh asked Arjun solicitously.

"Oh, before half an hour," Arjun said smilingly.

"Then, will you stay here alone?"

"That is no problem dad, you go and come back,"

"Okay then, we would be back soon,"

"Okay,"

"Then, Divya and I shall go, you rest here," saying thus Paresh went to his room.

Arjun closed the door and lay in the bed.

"Arjun says, he has a headache," Paresh told Divya when he changed his dress.

"Oh alas! Is it severe?" Divya asked worriedly.

"No. He asks us to go and be back soon,"

"Then, let him rest here,"

"Yeah, I told him to take rest,"

Paresh and Divya went to Arjun after sometime. They knocked at the door and Arjun opened the door.

"How are you now, Arjun? Has the headache decreased?" Divya asked Arjun as he opened the door.

"Yeah, somewhat," Arjun said smilingly.

"You don't come with us?"

"No mum," Arjun said as he called Divya thus.

"Then, you come and lock the door from inside after we went," Paresh told Arjun, later.

"Okay,"

Paresh and Divya walked to the portico when Arjun followed them, Arjun stood in the portico when Paresh and Divya went to their car and ascended it; he went to the gate and opened it for them, Paresh drove the car to the main road.

"Bye Arjun, rest until we come," Paresh said to Arjun on reaching the main road.

"Bye," Arjun said.

"Bye Arjun," Divya waved hands to him.

"Bye,"

Arjun came back to the house and then to his room. He just closed the front door of the house, he did not lock it. He sat in the chair and put his arms on the table and placed his head over them and remained in that position for long. He had been thinking to kill himself from the day, his mother died that he did not desire to live in the absence of her, but, he lived because his father was there; after the death of his father, he did not wish to live as his father was everything to him as his mother too was to him, Arjun did not wish to live in spite of all the love and caring of Paresh and Divya.

Now that, he has understood that it is Paresh who killed his father, Arjun's mind is burning with hatred and vengeance towards Paresh. He did not know what to do because Paresh has done this out of love for him and he thought what is happened is happened, Paresh cannot give his father back to him. Otherwise, he would have killed Paresh before he killed himself.

Arjun also felt sorry for Paresh that he is loving him very much that he cannot stand it if he died, the couple is blissful to get their son back. Arjun did not like to sadden them, but, he has no desire to live further. He cannot bear the anguishes of bereavement of his parents.

Arjun thought about Puja. He felt so sorry for her too that she would grieve much if she learns that he is dead. Arjun had loved her so dearly and she too back that he thought of not committing suicide lest she be woeful as he cerebrated about Paresh and Divya that they too would become very sad if he killed himself. Arjun remembered his relatives, friends and others, who also will be crestfallen if he killed himself. He remained in that position of sitting. Outside the house, it was cold. Sounds of dogs barking, cats meowing were heard. The neighbours and the people talking to each other in the nearby shop remained as they were earlier.

*   *   *   *   *

Paresh and Divya reached Irfan's residence. They went to the house after parking the car on the roadside. There were a number of people assembled over there in the yard of the house among whom, there were adults and children, who ate the food they took and talked among themselves; Paresh's friend, Irfan was there among the people to receive guests to whom Paresh and Divya walked, Irfan greeted them warmly when he saw them and asked them to sit as a lot of chairs were placed there, after inquiring them about their affairs. Paresh met many of his friends there and he chatted to them as Divya went to the inside of the abode.

Irfan's house was somewhat big, he is an engineer, working in Pune, he resided there and came home once in two weeks to his family, here. This is his son's wedding who works abroad. Many people came to the wedding as it had turned to be six thirty as the light bulbs which were there in plenty everywhere, outside and inside the house were turned on and they illumined brightly. After sometime, Paresh went to dine with his friends and he took Chicken Biriyani and fried chicken pieces as his friends too took Biriyani and other food items such as Roti and Butter nan along with mutton gravy and other items as it was a buffet. Paresh dined with his friends, he was thinking about Arjun who, as he thought, might be suffering from headache and he wished to return home soon.

After dining, Paresh met the bridegroom and talked to him. He was a well behaved youth who talked to Paresh politely and Paresh liked him very much; he was handsome and he looked more attractive in his wedding garment. Paresh met Irfan and told him that he wanted to quit early that Arjun is alone in the house and he is having a headache. It was only then, Irfan recalled Arjun and he inquired why he did not come to the wedding, he knew who Arjun was as Peresh had told him about Arjun and he had seen him when he went to Paresh's house to invite them to the wedding. When Irfan came to know that he is having a headache and that is why he did not come to the wedding, he asked Paresh to bring him to his house on another occasion. Paresh met Divya as he went inside the house and they took leave of Irfan, his wife and their children and later they returned home after saying goodbye to their acquaintances too.

"I think we are late, Arjun would be waiting for us," Paresh said as he drove the car.

"Yes, let us buy something for him," Divya said, looking at Paresh.

"Yeah, we can buy Broasted chicken, Tandoori chicken or something like that for him," Paresh said, looking at Divya.

Paresh stopped the vehicle afterwards when it reached in front of a restaurant.

"Let us buy something from here. Are you coming with me, Divya, or, are you sitting inside the car?" Paresh asked Divya.

"It may take some time to get the food, I too am coming with you," Divya said looking at the restaurant.

"Then come," Paresh said as he stepped out of the car.

Both Paresh and Divya went to the restaurant. Paresh asked the cashier whatever was there as food items and the man said, there are food items such as Tandoori chicken, Broasted chicken, beef chilly and chicken fry.

"Then, please give us one full Broasted chicken and buns," Paresh told the cashier.

"Okay, please sit there and wait for some minutes," the cashier said to Paresh and Divya politely, pointing to the chairs, which were there in a row.

"Okay," said Paresh and he and Divya sat there.

"Oh it is you, Paresh," Paresh turned to his left hearing his name being called.

"Oh Karthik, you," Paresh exclaimed, seeing his friend.

It was a neighbour and friend of Paresh. Paresh asked him to sit with him. Divya smiled to him as she knew him and he smiled to her back.

"Where are you coming from, Paresh?" Karthik asked Paresh smilingly.

"Oh, we are coming from a wedding of my friend's son," Paresh beamed as he said.

"Where is Arjun? Hasn't he come?" the man asked Paresh as he knew Arjun.

"No, he has not come, he is having a headache,"

"Oh I see,"

They talked and after sometime, a waiter came to them with Broasted chicken and buns and Paresh paid for the food.

"Karthik, are you on your way to home? If so, you can come with us," Paresh asked Karthik with a smile.

"No, thanks. Paresh, I will come later,"

"Then see you, bye,"

"Bye,"

Paresh and Divya went to their car, Paresh carried the plastic bag which contained the food. They ascended the car and it moved forward. Darkness had pervaded everywhere and Paresh turned on the lights and they could see things distinctly; all other drivers on the way had turned their lights on.

As they went further, Paresh made it out that there has occurred a traffic block. The vehicles are not moving forward and those coming hither, too have been blocked as a big tree had fallen to the road and it would take time for the traffic to be in former condition. Paresh inquired a boy about the traffic block and understood the reason for it.

"Divya, there is a traffic block. We will be late when we reach home." Paresh said to Divya anxiously, looking at her.

"You please call Arjun on the phone and tell him, we would be late," Divya said as if to soothe him.

Paresh took his mobile phone out of his pants pocket and dialled Arjun's number and waited for him to take the phone. Arjun's phone rang, but, there was no response as he did not take the phone.

"He doesn't take the phone," Paresh said to Divya as Arjun did not take the phone though it rang several times.

"You try again, may be, he must have fallen asleep,"

"Oh, that would be the reason then,"

Time passed and the vehicles began to move as the road has been cleared of the fallen tree. Paresh too took the vehicle forward like other drivers and after sometime he could drive speedily along the road.

Paresh and Divya reached their residence. Paresh sounded his horn to inform Arjun that they have come, but, Arjun did not come. Paresh sounded the horn again and again. They thought, he must be sleeping. Paresh descended from the car and opened the gate himself and took the car inside. They felt as if the door is not locked from inside when they looked at it.

CHAPTER 19

Paresh and Divya became discomposed as to why Arjun had not locked the door from inside. They alighted from the car swiftly and came to the portico and checked whether the door has been locked or not, and, they found it to be not locked.

"Why didn't Arjun lock the door, Divya?" Paresh asked Divya anxiously.

"He must have forgotten," said Divya as she opened the slightly opened door fully.

"Arjun...Arjun," Paresh went to Arjun's room, calling him.

Divya followed him. Both of them were on pins and needles that something must have happened to Arjun, Paresh knocked at the door but there was no response. He looked at Divya with a worried face, Divya too became worried.

The doorbell rang just then. Paresh and Divya went to see who has come, Paresh opened the door. Paresh was shocked to see a police inspector and two constables standing in the portico.

"Are you Paresh?" the inspector asked Paresh, smiling slightly.

"Yes, I am Paresh," Paresh said smiling, without showing his anxiety.

Divya did not know why the police has come to their residence. She looked at the inspector and smiled, the inspector was in a serious mood and he smiled slightly to Divya .

"Are you aware that your friend Ashok Kumar was murdered?" the inspector asked Paresh looking at him somberly.

Paresh looked at Divya and then to the inspector and said : "Yes,"

Divya looked at Paresh that she wondered why he told her a lie.

"How did you know?" the inspector asked again.

"I had gone there after the murder and knew from others," Paresh spoke without showing his apprehension outwardly.

"Had you any intention to kill Ashok Kumar?" the inspector asked Paresh frankly.

Paresh looked at Divya and then to the inspector with a slightly worried face. He did not say anything.

"Answer me, Paresh," the inspector looked seriously at Paresh as he said.

"Yes," Paresh told the inspector as he had not the courage to lie to the inspector.

"Why?"

"In order his son to regard me as his father,"

"Why?"

"I thought he is my son, that I had lost my son years ago and the boy resembled my son greatly,"

"So, you killed him to own his son,"

"Yes,"

"How did you kill him?"

"I shot him with my gun,"

"Have you licence to keep the gun?"

"Yes,"

"Show me your gun and licence,"

"I will bring now, you come and sit here," Paresh led the inspector and the constables to the guestroom.

The inspector and the constables sat in the guestroom. Divya brought them orange juice and snacks and stood near them very sadly, realising it was her husband, the cause of Ashok Kumar's death and she fretted, her husband would have to go to jail.

Paresh brought the gun and the licence and showed them to the inspector. The inspector examined them and placed them on the table.

"There is a witness who saw you shooting Ashok Kumar and that is why we came to you," the inspector looked at Paresh and said.

"Yes, I am so remorseful about that," Paresh uttered showing an expression of penitence on his face.

"When did you meet Ashok Kumar first?"

"More than a month ago. I met him when he was in Qatar,"

"You followed him when he came back to India?"

"Yes,"

"Hasn't his wife died?"

"Yes,"

"It is so cruel from your part to kill the father of a motherless child,"

Paresh did not speak. He bent his head down.

"Don't you know, you would have to go to jail?" the inspector asked after sometime.

"Yes,"

"Aren't you afraid?"

"Yes,"

"Okay, where is Ashok Kumar's son now?"

"He is with us, I adopted him. I am following the procedures for the adoption,"

"Is he now here with you?"

"Yes, he is in his room,"

"Call him,"

Paresh and Divya went to Arjun's room and knocked at the door and called him repeatedly. There was no answer. They went to the inspector and told him the matter. The inspector and the constables came to Arjun's room, the inspector knocked at the door but there was no response. Then, he tried to open the door by lowering the handle of the door. The door was not locked.

"This is not locked," the inspector said to Paresh with a smile.

"Yeah," Paresh said, simpering.

All of them entered the room, seeing Arjun sitting in the chair and putting his arms on the table and placing his head over it. They suspected, something has happened to him and Paresh and Divya called him several times, shaking him with their hands, but, Arjun did not wake up.

"Was he having any difficulty?" the inspector asked Paresh as he shook Arjun slightly.

"He had a headache," Paresh said with worried eyes.

"Had you gone anywhere leaving him here?"

"Yes, we had gone to a wedding and came back recently,"

"He remained here?"

"Yes,"

The inspector inspected Arjun as Paresh and Divya looked on.

"He has ceased breathing," the inspector said to Paresh and Divya.

"Oh my god!" Paresh could not believe that Arjun has died and he burst into tears.

Divya too wept. Both Paresh and Divya hugged Arjun and cried. They could not stand the grief and they cried loudly intermittently. The inspector and constables removed their caps and stood there and they consoled the couple.

The inspector found a small bottle of poison on the table and he showed it to Paresh and Divya.

"It is a suicide," the inspector said to Paresh and Divya and to the constables.

"Why did you do that, Deepak? Why did you do that?" Paresh wept, saying thus on hearing the inspector's words.

"Once you left us years ago and now too after finding you after years," Paresh continued saying as he sobbed.

Divya did not utter anything but she too was sobbing.

The inspector got the octavo in which Paresh had written remorsefully that he is the murder of Ashok Kumar, from among a lot of books that were on the table. He read what is written in it. The inspector felt sympathy for Paresh that he understood that Paresh is a poor man who did the murder out of love for Arjun and it would be so unfortunate for him to stay behind bars. Paresh saw the inspector reading the octavo, he made out that Arjun had read the book. He had not thought that Arjun would do this ghastly deed if he read the book. He wished, if he had not written thus in the book. Divya and the constables turned curious as to what would have been written in the book as they saw the inspector reading the book. The inspector handed over the book to Divya for her to read it, she cried after reading it. The constables too read the book and they felt commiseration for Paresh.

The inspector once again checked the octavo, he found something written in the book after four or five pages from the first two or three pages. He read it, it was written by Arjun. He wanted to know what Arjun has to say and he read the writing from the beginning. It read like this :

"My dear dad, Forgive me that I am leaving you forever. I had thought of killing myself from the moment I saw the cadaver of my mother and I did not wish to live at all after I saw my father dead. I wish to inform you that I am not your son, Deepak, which I knew when my father showed me my birth certificate. So, you should not grieve thinking on me. Tell mom to not grieve.

I feel very sorry for you that you would be jailed if police arrest you. I pray to God, let that not happen.

Do you know, I love a girl who is my classmate? Her name is Pooja. Please assuage her grief. Please console my friends and relatives.

I had loved you and mom very much and I know both of you loved me so dearly. Forgive me. I am going to my parents to heaven. I pray to God you to get your son, Deepak back. You should love me too in the next life.

I have nothing to write more. I am stopping. Yours Deepak."

The inspector's eyes got wet as he read the writing. Paresh, Divya and the constables made out that Arjun had written something in the book and they wanted to know what he has written; the inspector gave the book to Paresh and Paresh read what Arjun had written.

Paresh understood that Arjun is not his son and he lamented and he handed the book over to Divya and she too wept after reading it, the constables too read it and they felt sad.

"Paresh, now phone your relatives, friends and acquaintances and tell them about the death, so that, they can come and see the body," the inspector said to Paresh after minutes.

"Yes," Paresh said.

"You do whatever is needed after the death of someone, we want the body for post mortem afterwards," the inspector enunciated looking at Paresh in a serious manner.

"Yes sir," Paresh said.

Paresh called his relatives and acquaintances by phone and informed them about the death of Arjun. He told them that Arjun committed suicide and he said to them the cause of it.

After sometime, people began to reach the house and later, there was a multitude inside and outside of the house. Relatives placed Arjun's body on a bedstead for the peole to see it after washing it. Arjun's relatives, friends and acquaintances lamented to lose him forever.

People talked about the plight of Arjun, Paresh and Divya that they knew about all that happened between them, they felt it as a movie story. People came continuously to Paresh's house as they knew about the death of Arjun. They felt much sympathy for Paresh and Divya and they realised Arjun deserved great sympathy.

People turned to the outside of the house to the main road hearing a loud cry suddenly and many of them went to the outside, wanting to know what the matter is. They made out that it was a thief crying when the police hit him; the larcenist had been brought to them by a crowd, who caught him when he was attempting for burglary. People had seen earlier, the police jeep parked on the roadside and the inspector standing inside the house. The constables had returned to the jeep and the inspector remained in the house and the thief was brought to the constables.

People gathered around the police jeep and watched the robber who was wearing handcuff and resisting the constables' beating and who had been lashed by the people earlier before he was brought to the constables. The constables asked those who gathered there to move away from the thief who was sitting in the police jeep as he had been made ascend the jeep earlier, but, the people would not move back as there was rush with a lot of them.

Afterwards, the inspector came to the scene. The constables said to the inspector about the thief and he looked at him and asked the constables, from where he was caught and other things. Later, the inspector and the constables took the thief to the police station; the inspector had decided to return to Paresh's house later that he had to take the body to post mortem. After the police jeep moved, the people went to Paresh's house and remained there.

CHAPTER 20

The inspector questioned the thief at the police station. From his countenances and words, the inspector suspected that there is something mysterious about him, and so, he questioned the robber in detail.

"Did you steal anything?"

"No, I couldn't to,"

"When did you go there?"

"At 8 o' clock,"

"Did you enter the house?"

"No, I was trying to,"

The inspector understood that the purloiner is shivering, though he tried his best to conceal it.

"Why are you so afraid?" the inspector asked him.

"Nothing,"

"Tell the truth,"

"Nothing,"

"I will make you tell,"

"Nothing,"

The inspector hit the thief on his face as he was interrogating him at the lock up.

"I am not afraid, I did not do anything," the burglar sweared.

"Are you aware that a death occurred near that house?"

"Yes,"

"How did you know?"

"I heard people saying,"

"Had you gone there?"

"No,"

"Don't lie, there are witnesses who saw you going there," the inspector had known that a man was seen to be going to Paresh's house at about 7 o'clock that two men informed him when he was at Paresh's house.

"It was not I," the thief said with fear that he may be hit in the face for a second time.

"I will make you say,"

The housebreaker thought of surrendering that this man would not spare him. He began to confess that he would put the screws on him.

"I went there, seeing those dwelling there, going out. When I entered the portico, it must have become 7 o' clock that I waited till then, darkness to pervade. When I pushed the door, it opened as it was not locked. I thought, there was nobody in the house, but, when I opened a room, I saw a boy sitting in a chair putting his arms on the nearby table and placing his head over it,"

"Then, what did you do?"

"I feared that I would be caught and I decided to do him in,"

"Then?"

"I stealthily moved to find something to hit him on the head. I got a hammer from the kitchen and I hit him on the head with it. He did not make any noise and I thought he died instantly,"

"Did you hear that the boy had killed himself?"

"Yes, I heard and now I suspect that the boy had died already before I hit him,"

"If that is the case, you may escape punishment,"

The man said nothing, he bent his head down.

"You remain here, I will be back soon," saying thus, the inspector locked the lock up and came to his seat and sat there.

"Atul, come here," he called one of the constables.

"Yes sir," the constable attended the inspector.

"We have to go to Paresh's house with the ambulance to bring Arjun's body for post mortem,"

"Yes sir,"

The inspector went with two constables to Paresh's house in the police jeep, two of them remaining in the police station. An ambulance too was heading there as per the order of the inspector. They reached Paresh's house after sometime and the inspector ascended from the jeep and walked to the house. The news that the thief must have murdered Arjun had spread among the people by then and they all were impatient to know about that and they asked the inspector about that.

"Sir, is it that Arjun committed suicide or murdered?"

"The thief says, he had hit Arjun on the head, but I think he had killed himself before that,"

What Paresh wrote in the book and what Arjun wrote in it afterwards had spread among the people and they too thought it might be a suicide. They talked about it that they felt so sorry for Paresh and Arjun and also for Divya that she would also have to live without her husband and Arjun as Paresh might be going to gaol.

The inspector and the constables entered the house and the inspector informed Paresh and others, that they are taking the body with them for post mortem. The relatives of Arjun, Divya and Paresh were present there, some of them covered the body with a cloth and the constables took it to the ambulance as the people gathered there, cleared the way for them. The police jeep and the ambulance moved forward as the people looked on. The people remained there for more time talking among themselves and later, they began to break up after many of them taking leave of Paresh and Divya and consoling them. Many of the relatives remained there.

*   *   *   *   *

Puja lay on the bed lamenting Arjun's death. She could not believe that Arjun committed suicide; she thought, he could have thought of her. She understood that Arjun had loved his parents that much that was the reason, why he did himself in, even not thinking of her; or, is it that he hadn't loved her sincerely that he did not wish to live in this world, where she was there to love him . Pooja thought retrospectively about the days with Arjun, she had never felt that his love was insincere. She recalled the moment, she first loved him, it was when the classes began in eight standard and before that both of them had seen each other, but, had not spoken much to each other.

Puja could not go to Paresh's house and see Arjun's body because she had not known earlier that Arjun had committed suicide and she now waited his body to come after the post mortem in order to take part in the funeral. Pooja had loved Arjun very dearly that she wished to marry him and she was aware that he too wished to marry her, tears rolled down her cheeks as she cried with convulsive catching of the breath.

*   *   *   *   *

It is said among the people that it would take more than two days, Arjun's body to reach Paresh's house. People wanted to know, whether he was killed or he committed suicide and there was much sympathy and love for Arjun among the people and they felt compassion for Paresh too that it would be so tiresome for such a meek man as him to spend years in jail and they wished to rescue him. Later, Arjun's body came to Paresh's residence after two days from the day it had been taken to post mortem, in an ambulance and it was carried to the house.

Everybody could know the cause of the death that he was not killed but it was that he killed himself; doctors could find that the cause of the death is that poison had entered his body. People had known that Arjun is not Paresh's son from Arjun's writing that Ashok Kumar had shown him his birth certificate and they felt relieved, that, otherwise Paresh would be more saddened if he still believed that Arjun is his real son. It was a shock to all of them, the demises of Kaveri, Ashok Kumar and Arjun which happened in the same family and within short intervals.

Arjun's body was to be taken to the pyre. People came from all over and the house and its surroundings were filled with people. There were the relatives of Arjun, Paresh an Divya, the friends of Arjun, Ashok Kumar, Kaveri, Paresh and Divya and the natives among them. Many of the students and teachers of the school, in which Arjun studied came to Paresh's house and there were a multitude in the residence among whom, there were Pooja and Arjun's close friends who were very sad. They could be seen with wet eyes and they did not talk much among themselves.

It was 3 o' clock in the evening. Some of Arjun's relatives and some others lifted Arjun's body and they walked with others to a nearby ground; the people walked like a procession to the terrain. When they reached there, the pyre was ready that it had been formed earlier and the body was placed over it when the people looked on. Any one of the relatives of Arjun was to ignite the pyre as he had no parents and children. Ashok Kumar's eldest brother, Vishal kindled the pyre as he had come from Qatar, knowing about the death of Arjun.

The flames soared high as the people looked on, whose eyes got wet. There were Paresh, Divya, Pooja, Arjun's close friends and Arjun's relatives among them who grieved in the reality that Arjun is gone forever and they cannot see him anymore, others too felt sad to be not able to see the boy hereafter. Afterwards, everybody began to disperse that they walked back to Paresh's house. Everybody mourned that they lost three beloved ones from the same family and they prayed to God for their eternal peace.

Paresh closed the door of his room. He lay in the bed, holding the pillow with both his hands and touching his face on it. Though he suspected Arjun to be not his son, he was not ready to believe that, he still regarded him to be his son in his mind; he thought, Arjun must be lying that Ashok Kumar showed him his birth certificate in order to console him that he must have thought, he would be relieved if he knew that he is not his son. Paresh recalled the days with Deepak before he was lost that how near to his heart was he and how lovingly Deepak behaved to him.

Paresh remembered him fondling Deepak and buying him everything, he wanted. Deepak being their only son, Paresh and Divya had brought him up like a prince and he was to be going to school after he went to kindergarten. Paresh recollected the moments when they visited Taj Mahal and when Deepak disappeared, with sadness. He thought about the finding of Deepak after years at Qatar and remembered how happy he was then. Now that, his son has killed himself without thinking how sad his father would be.

Paresh thought about going to jail. He did not know what to do. He was aware either he would be hanged or he would be jailed and he preferred to be hanged that he did not wish to live without Deepak and desired to go to, where he went. He thought about Divya and felt sorry for her to lose her husband and son.

Divya too was lying in the bed isolated from others, she mourned to lose Arjun that she too had believed Arjun might be her son and had loved him very much. She too was remembering the days with Deepak and she too did not wish to live longer that she is deprived of her son and now, she is going to lose her husband too.

All the others, who were the relatives of Arjun, Paresh and Divya and their friends and natives thought about Arjun, Ashok Kumar, Kaveri, Paresh and Divya things like these and felt sad thinking about them. Ashok Kumar's brothers Vishal and Nikil were among them with their families.

After sometime, a police jeep came and stopped in front of the house and the inspector, who had come earlier, ascended from it and came to the house with whom there were two constables and inquired about Paresh. Arjun's uncle, Nikil went to Paresh's room and said he has been called by the police. Paresh got up from the bed and went to the inspector; Divya too came to the portico, hearing that police enquires about Paresh. The inspector handcuffed Paresh as all others looked on, everybody felt sympathy for Paresh. Divya embradced Paresh and cried. Others consoled Paresh that everything would be all right, some of them cuddled him. The inspector asked Paresh to come with them. Paresh looked at Divya and others and later, he walked to the police jeep with the inspector and the constables. People gathered around the police jeep and later, the jeep moved forward.

THE END